A Prelude to The Great King and the Seer
Published by Vellichor and More
https://jessicapietroart.wixsite.com/1234/

✿ Created with Vellum

A Prelude

A collection of short stories, prophecies, and indulgences introducing

The Great King and the Seer

Jessica Pietro

TABLE OF CONTENTS

FOREWORD

A note from the author:

Welcome, my friends, to the world of Arkaemor. In this book, you will find short stories, prophecy and song, and other details readers yearn for. I hope you enjoy the stories and pictures I've put together for you, including a bonus story that will not be made available on my Substack. You will only find it here!

I'm so pleased you were excited enough about this upcoming series to purchase *A Prelude*. If you haven't already, you might consider following me on Substack, where I will continue to post new short stories. For updates on new books, specials deals, and everything else involving The Great King and the Seer, feel free to follow my social media pages, which you can find links to here:

https://jessicapietroart.wixsite.com/1234/contact

This book is a snapshot of what will one day be an entire collection of songs, stories, creature guides, and all the other notes Iris Belamour keeps in her journal. Until then, here is a glimpse at the Five Kingdoms of Arkaemor. Enjoy.

Jessica Pietro

PART ONE

SHORT STORIES

Amaryllis and the Prince
Reaping 15, 4004

As the Reaping moon rose into the sky, Amaryllis used its light to better see her paint as she scraped it across the canvas. Firelight lit the room, but the white luminance of the full moon brought the picture to life.

She'd cracked a window to let the cold-season breeze tickle her skin. Though she would always prefer the jungle of Metsa Sateen, she thought spending the end of the year in Reginaterra might be a close second. It was the only territory with obvious seasonal changes. Savanni had a wet season and a dry season, but other than the crisping of the grasses and the growing grain in the farmlands, few differences could be seen. Grapes began to ripen near the end of Storm or early in the month of Ammil in the Grim Wilds, and more flowers bloomed over Petal than any other time in the Metsa.

None of that compared to the deciduous leaves of Reginaterra melting from green to crimson and saffron and amber, filling the forest outside her window in a blanket of wildfire. Then all the leaves would fall from the trees, and a new season of warmth would begin.

A soft knock followed the scuff of the door cracking open. Amaryllis looked out around her canvas to see Alexander's head peeking into her room.

"Ama?" he whispered. "Can I come in?"

"Of course, Prince Alexander. You are always welcome." She set her pallet on the stand next to her, though her brush continued its journey across the canvas.

Alexander scurried in and joined her by the window. "Wow! Where is this one?"

"What are you doing out of bed? I thought Alice took you to bathe an hour ago."

A mischievous grin curled his lips. "I snuck away. Don't tell on me, please Ama!"

Amaryllis tapped her knee, and he hopped into her lap with glee. "This is Lacuna Kaput. It's a waterfall in the rainforest. Isn't it lovely?"

"In Metsa Sateen? I think I know it." Alexander scratched his chin. "Oh! It's in that song you always sing me."

"That's right. Have you been practicing the words?"

He nodded and puffed up his chest. "I know almost all of them now, but I still mess them up sometimes. I haven't told anyone else, just like you said."

"Good boy."

"I like this painting." He pointed at the picture, his finger trailing the water falling from tree to lagoon. Then he looked at her. "Can I have it when it's finished? You let mama hang some of your paintings throughout Castle Solís, but I don't have one in my room yet."

Amaryllis shook her head. "This one has a greater purpose than gathering dust in a Prince's bedroom."

He giggled. "Okay, Ama."

Putting the brush in his hand, Amaryllis guided it around the canvas as she hummed the song about the Monastery of the Morrow. Alexander hummed along. When they reached the second to last verse, she sang the words out loud, and the Prince joined in.

All lands come together to repair a grand era,
Each used in the end to unlock the Elvyra.
A childson is needed to do the unbending,
To unwind the history and bring forth all mending.

To shred all to ruins, he'll forfeit his crown,
To rebuild the world, it must first be torn down.
When all is restored, all will bow to one Master,
Living in freedom; peace and joy ever after.

Alexander clapped quietly when they finished. "See, Ama? I remembered it!"

"Yes, you did." Amaryllis hugged him, rocking him back and forth until he laughed. Then she touched his chin so he looked at her. "You just keep repeating those words, okay? No matter what happens, no matter how big you grow, never forget them. Do you promise?" He nodded and returned his attention to the painting. Dipping her brush in magenta and orange, she added flowers to the outer edge of the cavern. "You know, Alexander, some day, I'll have little ones of my own."

His eyes widened, and he drew back his chin. "Really? How many?"

She tapped her lips with the end of her brush. "Two, maybe."

He considered that with a furrowed brow. "Will they be boys or girls?"

"I guess that's up to Elohim, isn't it?"

He looked up at her and whispered, "Ama, you said we aren't supposed to talk about Him."

She leaned closer and bopped his nose. "When it's just you and me, we can talk about Him all we like."

"Oh, right." Alexander relaxed into her, letting his head rest against her shoulder. His hand lifted to her hair, twisting a lock around his finger. "Well, I hope they're boys. Because girls are gross."

Amaryllis laughed. "Prince Alexander, how could you say such a thing? Girls are radiant and lovely and wonderful." He stuck a finger down his throat, and she threw her head back with mirth. "Well, whether or not I have girls or boys, you'll help me look after them, won't you?"

Nodding, he turned to the side and let his eyes fall close. "Yes, Ama. I'll help you look after them. But I'm still going to ask Elohim to give you boys."

"That's fine." She kissed his forehead and continued painting. A few minutes later, another knock sounded at the door. Alexander stiffened as Amaryllis called, "Come in, Alice."

Alice walked in with a smile. "I knew you would be in here, Prince Alexander. You know it's well past your bedtime. Come along." She held out her hand.

Alexander sighed. "Time for me to go, Ama. Thanks for letting me paint. Merry night and merry dreams." He kissed her on the cheek before sliding from her knee.

Pulling him into a hug, she rustled his hair. "You are magnificent, Alexander. I'll see you tomorrow. Merry night and merry dreams."

THE MAD KING

WILLOW, 1923

The sun had already begun to set over the mountains when Ingrid at last pulled herself away from the gardens. Sage had come twice in the past hour to let her know dinner was ready to be served. When she entered the hall, she called, "I am here, Sage. Sorry to have kept you." She slid the fur coat from her shoulders, and Sage hurried to take it.

"It was no trouble, my lady. Leopold kept your dinner warm." Leading her to the dining room, Sage rounded the table to pull out her lady's chair. "Did you enjoy your time in the gardens?"

"I always enjoy my time in the gardens."

After peeking into the kitchens to let the cook know of Ingrid's arrival, Sage retrieved a goblet from the rack and unstoppered the cork from the wine. "The roses are looking lovely this year. I haven't seen you grow violet ones before."

"Thank you, Sage. The seeds were a gift from Edith, the butcher's wife." Ingrid laid a napkin in her lap as a man entered the room and sat a steaming plate before her. A farmer had gifted the household two chickens that afternoon, and one had been roasted for the evening meal. "Thank you, Leopold. I'd like a second plate, if you please."

The cook glanced at Sage, his brow wrinkled into a frown.

Sage curtsied. "Oh, that won't be necessary, my lady."

"Please, I insist. I would prefer not to eat alone tonight. It is no bother, is it Leo?" Ingrid looked back and forth between them, smiling when Leopold sighed and returned to the kitchen. Gesturing to the seat across from her, she said, "Sit?"

Sage pulled out the chair and sat down. "You know he hates it when you do this."

"Yes, I know. But is he the master of this house? Or am I?"

"You are, my lady."

Leopold returned with a second plate and set it in front of Sage. Then he left with a huff that made both women chuckle.

Sage bit into the chicken leg and hummed. "This is divine."

Ingrid took a bite, too, washing it down with a sip of wine. "*This* is divine. It's imported from the Grim Wilds, you know. A friend sent it to me."

"I know, my lady. And I know which friend you speak of, too." Sage accepted the offered goblet and took a taste.

"I cannot imagine what your tone is implying, Sage." Ingrid lifted a brow before rising to pour Sage her own glass. They continued on with their meal, conversing lightly about the day and the week to come. Ingrid planned to travel into town the following morning with the intention of visiting the tailor and ordering some new clothes. Sage said she might spend the evening away from the mansion, if her lady didn't mind. Then she told Ingrid about the man she'd met in the market, and how handsome and kind he'd been.

An anxious knock at the door had their eyes meeting. The lady's maid stood, but Ingrid said, "Let me. You keep eating."

"But, my lady, I—"

Ingrid waved away her protests and left the room. Another knock had her quickening her pace down the hall. When she reached the door, her fingers paused on the handle. Pounding on the opposite side startled her, and she pulled it open to find a man, prone on the ground with his head leaned against the jamb. "Valerian?"

The man grinned up at her as though nothing were amiss. "Ingrid, lovely evening, wouldn't you agree? I do love the Cordilleran sky." A hacking cough drew his hand to his chest and blood from his mouth.

"What in the world happened to you?" Ingrid knelt next to him, already wiping blood from his cheeks with her dress.

"Don't soil such a lovely outfit on my account." He pushed her hands away and used his own sleeve to catch the blood from another cough. "Though I suppose when it's soiled, you'll need to take it off, and wouldn't that be a fine sight for a wounded man to behold."

Ingrid glared at him. "Everything is jest and madness with you. Come on." She lifted him from beneath his arms and helped him stand. On his feet, he leaned against the door as she pulled his arm across her shoulder.

Sage appeared in the hall, stopping short when she saw the mess. Valerian said her name in greeting, and she replied, "You're bleeding all over the rug."

Ingrid said, "Nevermind that. Retrieve warm water and a rag. We will be in the drawing room."

"Yes, my lady. Shall I summon Leo?"

Ingrid shook her head. "I can manage him alone. Thank you, Sage." She pulled Valerian closer so his weight rested against her as they walked the hall. "Do you plan to explain? Or is this to be another of your misadventures?"

Valerian chuckled. "I shall explain when I've had some wine." He raised his voice. "Sage! Bring along that wine I sent, will you, dear?" Sage shouted back an irritated reply.

"She is not pleased with you."

"That makes it all the more entertaining." Valerian coughed again as Ingrid lowered him to the lounge.

When he stretched his legs out, she sat next to him and leaned closer, lifting a hand to his cheek. "Let me look at you." A gash above his eye dripped blood down his face. Another on his neck had the collar of his shirt marred red.

"Look all you like."

She prodded the skin above the deepest wound. "Shall I take care of this for you?"

Valerian groaned as he attempted to find a comfortable position. "Leave it. Let it be a reminder of why I did it."

Ingrid met his gaze. "Did what?"

He smiled and reached for her. "Have you always had these black streaks in your hair?"

Sage returned with a bowl of water, and Ingrid thanked her. "Is there anything else you require, my lady?"

"The wine?" Valerian asked.

Sage glared at him. "It's gone." When she left the room, Ingrid wet the rag and began cleaning his face.

Valerian sucked air through his teeth. "It's cold."

Ingrid smiled as she rang blood from the rag. She wiped his neck, unbuttoning the top two buttons of his shirt. His cuffs had been rolled to his elbows, revealing wounds on his arms. "What did she do to you, Valerian? And why? This is horrible."

He slid a hand behind his head, propping it up. "I left her, Ingrid."

Ingrid's breath caught in her throat, her hand pausing midair. "What do you mean?"

"I left. After everything that happened with Erys, things have gotten so out of hand. And I just…" His eyes slid from hers. "I couldn't be a part of it anymore."

Her mind reeled with implications as she looked him over. She busied her hands, brushing silver hair from his forehead to clean away splattered blood. "What will you do now? Where will you go?"

He smiled. "Well, I came here. You assured me the door would always be open, did you not?"

Ingrid cleared her throat and stood, dropping the rag into the bowl. "Indeed, I did."

He tried to lean forward, but it pained him too greatly. "You need not run from me, Ingrid. I am not the man I once was. At least, I endeavor not to be."

She nodded. "That man would not have left. She is angry?"

Looking down at himself, he shrugged. "I think that's a fair assessment. She doesn't know I came here, though. We should be safe for now."

"She might. Does this mean you have given up your crown? That you would leave your people under her rule alone?"

Valerian forced his body up, sliding his feet to the floor with his elbows on his knees. "What would you have me do, Ingrid? What would you do?"

"I don't know." She backed away until she hit the wall, her eyes never leaving his.

"Perhaps, in time, I can make amends for all my sins. Perhaps someday I will take back the Thrones of Arkaemor and rule this world again, without her at my side. Then I can do things differently than she and I did together."

"Perhaps. I will have Sage make up a room for you. Or maybe Andrew. Sage may put a snake in your bed."

"Does Cordillera have snakes?" He quirked a brow, and the movement made him wince.

"*Huge* snakes." She smiled, and he returned it.

"I appreciate your kindness, old friend. More than you know."

"We will speak again in the morning. Merry night, Valerian." Ingrid slipped from the room before he could reply and bumped into Sage in the hall. Taking her hand, she pulled her up the stairs to ensure their guest couldn't overhear.

"What is he doing here?" Sage closed the door to Ingrid's chambers and let her back rest against it.

Ingrid sat on the bed. "He says he left her. He needs a place to stay while he sorts out what to do next. Have Andrew make up a room for him, will you?"

"Of course, my lady, but how are you?"

Ingrid's hand rose to her heart. "I am…well, I don't quite know. What does it mean that he came here? Surely there are others he could have turned to. He and Decha have long been allies. Would he not have been better suited to handle this?"

"He trusts you."

"But why, I cannot say." Ingrid's eyes scoured the rug as her mind processed the events of the evening and all the possible futures that lay ahead of them. He'd left before, but something about him seemed different this time. In the past, he'd been emotional, making the decision in anger and returning home when his temper abated. This time he seemed…content. Settled in his decision, wherever the path may lead.

"Because you are kind, my lady. A treasure to your people, a gift to your friends, a blessing to me." Sage smiled. "You know I have never much cared for the man, but if he is here, perhaps he seeks what resides in there." She pointed, and Ingrid looked down at the hand covering her heart. "Though he also might be seeking the rest of it." Sage gestured to her entire body, and Ingrid blushed. "Either way, it is better for the world if he and Sirena have parted ways, is it not? Imagine how different Arkaemor could be if you tame the Mad King."

"You should not speak like that. I have no intention of taming him. He is not here for romance, nor is he in search of a new queen. And even if he were, he is not the kind of man I wish to find myself linked to for eternity. I have seen far too much of his heartlessness to ever trust him so deeply."

Sage lifted a shoulder. "I will speak to Andrew. Then I'll return to help you change for bed."

C

When Ingrid woke the following morning, she dressed and made her way to the dining room for breakfast.

Sage sat at the table drinking a mug of coffee. A fire had already been lit in the hearth. "Come sit, my lady. I'll pour you some coffee." Setting her book face down on the table, she rose but stalled as Ingrid lifted a hand.

"I am quite capable, Sage. Thank you." Ingrid strode the length of the table and began fixing herself a drink.

Sage put the mark in her book and closed it, setting it aside before pulling her knees to her chest and tightening the blanket wrapped around her shoulders. "It's so cold today. The snow has been falling heavily all night."

"Thank you for lighting the fire." Stirring in a spoonful of sugar, she thought of the woman who'd gifted it to her in exchange for some advice about dealing with pesky orädi. The people of Villa Montis were always giving her things, despite her avid protests.

"I lit the one in the drawing room, too. It seems our guest never made it upstairs."

Ingrid paused her stirring. "He didn't?"

Sage shook her head. "I checked though, and he's still breathing. At least he was when I lit the fire, though anything is possible." She hid a grin with her mug.

"Very amusing, Sage." Ingrid pulled out the chair across from her and sat down. "Rather than visiting the tailor today, I think I'll go into town to purchase him some attire and return promptly. He does not seem to have packed a bag, and the suit he wears now is drenched."

"He looked to have left in a rush. But you shouldn't go, my lady. The snow is thick. Let myself or Andrew go for you. Especially if your creative eye is unneeded at the tailor, there is no reason to subject yourself to the poor weather."

Ingrid's head turned toward the window where the snow continued to fall in clustered flakes. "I will be fine. I should like the fresh air."

"Then take a stroll around the gardens."

Ingrid looked at her scoldingly, and Sage held up her hands in surrender. "I will go soon, before it gets worse. Should I check on him before I leave?"

"Do you *want* to check on him before you leave?"

Ingrid furrowed her brow and stood. "I would like breakfast for us both when I return."

"I'll let Leopold know." Sage lifted her mug in farewell.

Ingrid dipped her head and left the room. Her fur coat remained in the hall with her boots, and she tugged them on before braving the cold. When she returned over an hour later, she carried not only a bag of clothing for Valerian, but also five turnips, a new blend of tea leaves, and half a sugared ham. Setting the food on the dining table, she called for Leopold to retrieve it. Then she poured another mug of coffee and made her way to the drawing room.

Valerian snoozed on the lounge. Ingrid put the coffee on the table next to him and added another log to the fire. Digging through the bag of clothes, she pulled out a pair of pants and a button down shirt the color of the sky in its current state—a gray that matched his hair.

Valerian's yawning stretch turned into a groan as he was reminded of his injuries. He swore and tried to sit up, but every inch of his body felt stiff and sore.

Ingrid knelt on the floor next to him. "Merry morning."

When he saw her, he smiled, his eyes lighting up with surprise. Then he looked around, and memories of the previous day resurfaced. "Ah, yes. The pain makes sense now. I'd thought it all a bad dream." He returned his attention to her, and his smile widened. "And this a rather good one."

"There is coffee next to you, if you'd like. Why did you stay down here? I told you I would have Andrew make up a room."

"I believe I attempted to stand, and it became too trying a task." His sleepy eyes seemed to sparkle as they swept over her. "You look lovely in the morning, Ingrid."

She rose and retrieved the clothing from the table, setting them next to him. "You are incorrigible always, Valerian."

He chuckled. "It's one of my many charms. Where did you get the clothes? Do I have Andrew to thank for that as well?"

"I traveled to Villa Montis before you awoke."

"Ingrid, you didn't have to do that. I'll pay back whatever they cost."

"The townsfolk rarely allow me to pay for things. I will send them a few *terras* later today to cover it, but you needn't concern yourself. I'm happy to help." She sat down in a chair across from him and gave her attention to pressing wrinkles from her dress.

Valerian tried to sit up and groaned again, letting his head fall over the back of the lounge. "This is horribly uncomfortable."

"I can help you upstairs to your room. Perhaps the bed would suit you better."

He reached for his coffee and blew away the steam. "As much as I would delight in you taking me to bed, my body would be coming with me, so the discomfort would persist."

Her eyes flashed to his. "It's your stubbornness that's persistent."

"Another charming quality, I think."

Ingrid rolled her eyes and sighed. "You think very highly of yourself, as always. Perhaps you are not so changed as you wish to be."

Valerian pouted. "Your words cut deeper than my wounds, sweet Ingrid."

"Your words are like poison, as they always have been." Ingrid left the room, ignoring him as he called after her. Her heart raced with irritation, and Sage found her in the hall leaning against the wall with panicked breath.

"My lady? What happened?"

"He is as arrogant and full of himself as he was the day we left and every day since. How can a man lacking humility truly see the error of his ways? When he is healed, we will find him somewhere else to stay." Before Sage could respond, Ingrid rounded the banister and hurried up the staircase.

Sage listened until she heard Ingrid's bedroom door close, then she followed the hall to the drawing room and stopped in the doorway. Valerian seemed to be trying to stand. "I hope you plan on replacing that lounge, as well as the carpet by the door. Not even Andrew will be able to clean away these stains."

Chuckling amongst his wheezing, he said, "Of course. Anything you wish." He sat against the arm, letting himself rest before trying to move again. Then he took a sip of his coffee and stared at her over the mug.

"Okay, then I wish for you to leave. Nothing good will come of you being here. Not only do you bring with you the dangers of Sirena's wrath, but I fear you will break my lady's heart. It is no fragile thing, but she is too kind to turn you away, despite the vile beast we all know you to be."

Valerian smiled and sipped from his mug before returning it to the table. Bells from the clock on the mantle chimed the hour as he rose unsteadily to his feet. "I've always admired that sharp tongue, Sage. And while I appreciate your honesty, I'll be staying as long as Ingrid allows."

"Then I shall have to convince her otherwise." Sage crossed her arms, and he pushed off from the lounge, hobbling toward her.

"Then it will be a battle of wills, it seems."

"Why? Why drag her into this?"

"As you say, she is no fragile thing." Stopping next to her in the doorway, he braced himself with a hand on the frame.

"You know she cares for you, and you take advantage. That's who you are."

He chuckled and leaned in so his head hovered above her shoulder. "I shall endeavor to earn your trust as well, Sage. But know this: I have no intention of leaving."

C

As the sun rose and fell, rose and fell, and rose again, the recent barrage of snow settled into a light flurry. Ingrid returned to the garden after luncheon to check on her roses and tend to the weeds. Ivy dripped from the awning over the back porch, walling it in on either side.

Valerian stood against the post holding up the awning, blending into the wall of ivy so he remained out of sight until he chose not to be. He watched Ingrid trimming back bushes of violet roses, chuckling as the mischievous orädi got in her way.

"You are supposed to be helping, you know. Tricksy little monsters." She lifted a brow at the glowing creature digging a hole in the flower bed, and it tinkled in response. With the wave of her hand, she shooed it away. "If you're going to be destructive, then I have no need of you today." Another tinkle sounded, and the orb of light zipped away. Moments later, it peeked its head out around a nearby juniper and sent a flurry of white lights toward the roses. Ingrid smiled as the flowers bloomed in response to the orädi's magic. Glancing back over her shoulder, she said, "Thank you, friend. That's much better."

"You're even kind to the crag tricksters, I see. I suppose there's hope for me yet." Valerian's words startled her, catching her breath. When he stepped out from beneath the awning, she exhaled.

"Valerian, I did not see you standing there."

"Apologies, my lady. I didn't mean to scare you."

Ingrid stood and shook snow from her skirt. "I get lost out here sometimes. It is no fault of yours. Did you need something? You seem to be standing more securely today."

"All thanks to your generosity." He walked toward her, stopping a few paces away. "I must say, you look glorious right now: flushed from the cold, violet roses in your backdrop."

"If you cannot keep your compliments to yourself, then I'd prefer you not speak at all." Ingrid's eyes scoured the ivy behind him, avoiding his gaze. Taking advantage of her averted attention, Valerian stepped closer and was met with a dagger at his throat. He froze in alarm and held up his hands. "I would also prefer you keep your distance. Your hands are as duplicitous as your compliments."

Grinning, his lips broke open to reveal teeth. "You are quite a terrifying woman, Ingrid."

"It would serve you well to remember that."

Gray eyes flickered back and forth between hers. "Have dinner with me."

In her surprise, her grip loosened on the blade. "What?"

"I'm tired of eating alone in my room. Now that I've managed to make it back down the stairs, I'd like to repay you for your hospitality."

The dagger fell to her side. "I appreciate the thought, but it is not necessary."

Again he took a step closer, braving the fury of her weapon. "Then let it be merely a dinner among old friends, and not a payment. We are still friends, aren't we, Ingrid?"

"Of course we are, though it has not always been to my benefit."

The corner of his lips lifted as a cluster of snow landed on her cheek. His hand rose to wipe it away but stalled midair and slid around his back instead. "Tonight then? It's been ages since I've seen the full moon in Cordillera." He looked up, though the Willow moon was not yet visible in the sky.

Ingrid sighed. "As you wish. I'll have Leopold serve us on the rooftop balcony."

"Let me handle Leo. You relax. I'll take care of everything." He seemed to bubble with excitement that had Ingrid shaking her head and stepping past him on her way back to the house. Before she disappeared beneath the ivy, Valerian called after her, "See you tonight."

When Ingrid returned to her room later that evening to change for dinner, she found a dress she hadn't seen before hanging from her closet door. An envelope had been tucked into one of the folds, and she tugged it free. Holding it in the candlelight, she read:

> Sweet Ingrid,
> I am greatly looking forward to our moonlit dinner. Let this dress be an expression of my gratitude for all you've done for me.
>
> Vali

Sage entered soon after and moved to stand next to her in front of the dress. "He has style, I'll give him that."

Ingrid handed over the letter. "He is pushy and…" Her fingers trailed the fabric of the dress, heavy like wool but with an elegant fit. It was the color of the night sky: blue, like a sapphire, with white fur around the edges and silver embroidery. Atop lay a stole made from the pelt of an arctic wolf. "Manipulative."

"So deny his request. Show him you cannot be bought."

Ingrid looked at her. "I do like this stole, though." Sage chuckled and pulled it from the hanger, ushering Ingrid to the looking glass. Wrapping it about her shoulders, Sage stepped out of the way so her lady could get a good look at herself. It was a full pelt, with a head empty of its skull laying over her heart. "It's magnificent."

"So don't deny his request, and join him for dinner."

Ingrid laughed. "It seems such a simple thing, and yet, it is undoubtedly complicated."

Sage adjusted the stole, straightening her lady's dress beneath it so it lay right. "Because you love him?"

Ingrid caught her gaze in the reflection. "No."

Sage smiled knowingly. "Because you have *always* loved him."

Ingrid shook her head and returned her attention to her own reflection in the glass. "Because he is married to Sirena. He is her King, not mine. A fight may have torn them apart, but they have always fought. They are both like fire, and together, a raging furnace that will burn the world. He will go back to her, to his throne. His heart seeks that power more than anything else, no matter what she puts him through. It is why they led us to this freedom at the start. It is why they cut Erys from his throne. It is the reason for everything. He will never give up the Thrones of Arkaemor."

"Perhaps true love can change his heart."

"Perhaps obtaining his love will break mine." Ingrid pet the stole, feeling the soft fur with the tips of her fingers. Then she pulled it from her shoulders and held it between them. "I should return this now and be done with it."

Sage draped it over her arm. "It's up to you, my lady."

Ingrid faced the dress, thinking the deep blue would pair well with her skin. She touched it again, running her fingers along the intricate embroidery and silky ribbons. "Yes, return them both. Tell him I am not feeling well and need to postpone our dinner." She turned and pulled her nightgown from the rack.

Sage nodded and moved to help unfasten her corset. Then Ingrid slid into bed with a book in hand, and though she claimed to be fine, Sage thought she looked terribly sad. She carried the dress and pelt down the hall to the room Andrew had made up for their guest, and he opened the door after one knock. "You're moving quite fast for one so injured."

Valerian looked at the clothing in her hands. "I was already standing by the door. She doesn't like the dress?"

"My lady isn't feeling well this evening. She sends her deepest apologies." Sage extended the dress toward him.

"If she were merely ill, she would not be returning the gift, but saving it for a later time." He gestured to the garments in her hands, but didn't take them. "Have I done something wrong?"

Sighing, she let her arm fall to her side. "You being here is wrong, Valerian. You don't belong in Cordillera."

Valerian gave a single, slow nod of understanding. "She doesn't trust me."

"Would you?"

Raking a hand through his hair, he exhaled a heavy breath. "No, I suppose not. Tell her to keep the dress. I don't think it's my color." He closed the door before she could reply.

"Fine. *I'll* keep the dress." Sage held it to her body as if to test its fit. Then she sighed again and carried it to her room.

$$C$$

Over the next month, Valerian grew accustomed to life at the mansion. Though his charm never ceased, his obvious attempts at wooing her had. No more dresses arrived at her door, nor did he propose another moonlit dinner. Most evenings, he dined with her in the hall. At Ingrid's request, and to Leopold's great irritation, Sage often joined them. Ingrid insisted it felt less intense when it was the three of them, mostly because Sage and Valerian bickered constantly, so his attention remained on her.

During the day, he alternated between lingering nearby and keeping his distance. Ingrid showed him Villa Montis, her gardens, and her favorite path up the mountain. He showed her that even a king could chop wood for a fire, shovel snow, and clean the house.

One afternoon, Ingrid sat in the newly purchased lounge reading a book about a boy who pulled a sword from a stone, and Valerian balanced on a stool, buffing the chandelier with a feather duster. She watched him from the corner of her eye, hiding her amusement behind the velvet cover. Feeling her stare, he looked back at her, and the movement sent him toppling to the floor. Ingrid startled and sat up. When he appeared uninjured, she stopped restraining her laughter.

Valerian looked at her like she'd gone mad. "I am astonished, sweet Ingrid. I had no idea you could be so cruel."

She covered her mouth with her hand, pulling her feet beneath her and letting her book come to rest in her lap. "I was only thinking that this is why kings hire servants to dust."

His body relaxed against the rug. "Indeed."

"Sage would have died if she'd witnessed that."

"Shall we summon her, then? I could do it again."

Ingrid smiled. "Now who's being cruel?"

"She loathes me." Valerian rose to sitting, letting his upper body rest on his hands. "Has she always loathed me or is it a new development? I'm not sure I ever noticed one way or the other."

"She's protective of me." Ingrid looked down at her book, her fingers absentmindedly caressing the cover.

"And she thinks I might murder you in your sleep? Claim this mansion as my own? She can't believe her attitude would prevent that. Why, I would just do away with her first, wouldn't I?"

"She worries you will do far worse than that, Vali."

Valerian hummed. "Oh, I do like the sound of that."

Lifting her eyes to him, she furrowed her brow. "What?"

"You calling me *Vali*. It's far easier to say than Valerian, don't you agree?"

She lifted a shoulder. "It is not very kingly."

He mirrored her movement and winked. "Then it's lucky I'm no longer a king."

Ingrid sighed, setting her book on the table as she reached for her hot tea. It had a wonderful flavor, like cinnamon and cloves. "One does not simply stop being a king."

"No, there is certainly nothing simple about it. Is that why you keep your distance from me? You fear I will return to my throne?"

"Since you still refer to it as *your* throne, I think the odds are likely."

Chuckling, Valerian rose from the floor and sat next to her on the edge of the lounge. "It is true, I do seek the power that comes with kingship. Maybe I will have it again some day, but I will never again rule next to Sirena. I can't. She's horrible. I was horrible, too, but I can't stomach her brutality anymore. Erys was her brother. She loved him more than all of us, even me. Yet she betrayed him, ensnared him in eternal torment, as she has with so many others. Not only that, she used me to help her do it. My eyes have been opened, Ingrid, and I can no longer sit idly by and watch her tear this world apart."

Ingrid pulled her legs closer, making room for him to sit properly. "It is a great speech, but is it truth?"

Valerian leaned back, propping his ankle over his knee. "It is as true as anything I have ever known. I won't lie to you, Ingrid. I do hope to have someone at my side as I fight back. The journey will be long and littered with trials, none greater than putting up with me and my stunning personality." He grinned, his brow raised. "I'm not asking for your love, only your heart, your strength, your guidance. I ask for your companionship. I'm sure to need a level head at my side. Help me take her down once and for all. Won't you?"

Ingrid exhaled a tight breath, thinking it over as she ran a finger around the edge of her mug. She looked at him, his relaxed posture, his confident smile. "But Vali, you know what the prophets have been saying, do you not? Surely their words reached you in Reginaterra. The servants seeking truth, connected to Elohim himself."

"The navi." He nodded, his eyes elsewhere. "Without them, Erys would remain."

"Indeed. So then you must know that we have no hope of beating Sirena until the woman in white arrives."

"Hair like the snow that crowns these mountaintops." Valerian ran a hand through his own hair, pushing it off his forehead. Despite the lack of wrinkles on his face, his hair was such a light gray it looked almost white, but not nearly as white as the snow. "Then let us prepare the way for her. Let us build an army, a kingdom—whatever we can do to make her success possible. And what better place to do it than amongst the snow-caps the prophets compare her to?"

Ingrid took another sip of her tea before setting it down on the table and turning to face him with her elbow on the back of the lounge. "Villa Montis is far different from Inaravale, Vali. I am not their queen."

He purred with relish. "Have I mentioned how much I adore your accent, Ingrid? It might be the most beautiful thing I've ever heard." One side of his lips curled, and as he tilted his head, hair flipped over his part making it stand straight up. "You could be their queen, you know. They already love you."

She shook her head. "You are not the kind of king they would seek. You are not the kind of king I wish to see ruling over them. They are a gentle people, peaceful and hardworking. Proud."

Sliding from the lounge, he dropped to his knees before her. "Then teach me."

Ingrid scoffed. "Teach you what? How to be a king? Have you not spent years with a crown on your head?"

"Indeed I have, and I've done an atrocious job, haven't I? And so, my sweet Ingrid, will you stand with me? Will you help me raise a kingdom for when the white-haired maiden arrives?" He took her hand in both of his. "Will you teach me, Ingrid, to be the kind of king your people deserve?"

COMMANDER OF THE KING'S LEGION

LIVIANA 3, 4020

"I see six men patrolling by the front door. Four rifles, two blades. There's sure to be others nearby, as well as inside." Jax pulled his head from around the corner and pressed his back against the wall, eyes squinting as he lifted them to the sky. He'd never minded the sun and sand of the Grim Wilds except when layered up in High Legion battle gear.

"Easily dealt with." Hector checked his mag and glanced at Dagon as he holstered the pistol. "You ready, Wraith?"

"To toss out rebel trash? Always, General." Dagon's grin revealed both his crooked teeth and his innate malice. He looked across the alley and signaled with his hand for the other soldiers in crimson and gray to move forward. Then he, Jax, and Hector followed.

The company easily subdued the guards outside the governor's mansion. Many of the rebels were untrained civilians carrying weapons they didn't know how to use. Two more arrived around the western corner of the building. Hector knocked the first man's pistol free with the hilt of his sword before catching the woman's blade against his own. She hardened her features, but her eyes betrayed her. He had her on her knees in three swings. Jax tied her wrists behind her back, and Amar dragged her away to line her up with the others.

Jax wiped sweat from his brow and gestured to the door. Hector nodded. Then shouts drew their eyes back to the street. A horde of civilians carrying all manner of firearms, blades, and makeshift weapons charged toward them. A battle ensued. Clashing swords and shotgun blasts filled the courtyard. More rebel soldiers poured from the mansion.

Jax pulled Hector out of the line of fire and shot his attacker. Then he motioned again to the door. "Wraith can handle this. We should press forward."

"Let's go," Hector agreed. He shouted Dagon's name so he knew to take over command, and he and Jax slipped into the mansion. The heavy door instantly muffled the sounds of warfare. Having been in the governor's mansion before, Hector knew the way. He lifted his sword and moved deeper into the room. Jax followed, pistol raised.

The Grim Wilds had no sovereign over all, but Dysmaa remained one of the few cities in the territory with a governor, making it prime real estate for rebel takeovers. This wasn't the first, and Hector felt certain it wouldn't be the last.

The desire to overthrow the current governor came as no surprise as they walked the mansion halls. By the looks of it, he cared little about sharing his wealth with his people. Though not an extremely poor city, it was mediocre compared to Inaravale or Aeonian. Even Sal. They'd seen signs of poverty as they made their way to the city's center, but in the mansion, emerald tile covered the floors and glass windows offered protection from sandstorms.

Two rebels met them at a cross hall and were quickly dealt with. Jax tied their wrists and leaned them against the wall. "They're practically kids. He overthrew Dysmaa with rebel youths?"

"He must have other soldiers elsewhere." Hector peered down the hall and waited to see if anyone else was coming before waving Jax on.

"Not guarding the mansion, though? Where else would they be?"

Hector shrugged and held a finger to his lips as they approached the door to the governor's office. Jax moved to the opposite side and let his fingers rest on the handle. When Hector gave the signal, he threw it open, and both men charged in.

A large chamber with high ceilings, the governor's office had a long table stretching down its center and a desk at the far end. Behind the desk, a man with dark hair lounged in the governor's chair surrounded by armed guards. The previous governor's corpse lay next to them on the floor.

"*Nanma sha, sajjabo.*" The man seated at the desk grinned.

"Playtime is over, Ha Zan," Hector replied in Bryä.

Ha Zan shared a glance with those surrounding him. "*Kyah ahmpa* Bryä?"

"Yes, I do, but my friend isn't as fluent, so let's stick to Arkaen, shall we?"

The rebels chuckled, and Ha Zan looked pitifully at Jax before replying in Arkaen. "I suppose we can, but it is such a filthy language, is it not?"

"It's the language of the world." Jax scanned the room while tugging at his collar, wondering at the closed windows. It was sweltering in there without the breeze the tilted windows had offered in the hall.

"A world ruled by abominations." He shined the blade of his sword with a white cloth. "Bryä was a marvelous king, but he too was cut down like so many others."

Hector took a step closer, and the rebels flinched, each gripping their weapons tighter. "He thought himself so high as to create a language all his own, and then he lost his kingdom to rebel forces like you, or so the legends say. Regardless, the Wilds are *terra nullius* now and have been for centuries. Is it your intention to change that, oh great and powerful Ha Zan?"

"The Grim Wilds have never truly been unclaimed land, only unclaimed by Pollux and Sirena Aldrich. Here in the desert, we exist outside their ruthlessness and boundaries. A world all our own."

Jax chuckled. "The governors are elected by the people, but candidates are chosen by the royals of Arkaemor. The cities are occupied by Legion soldiers. King or no king, you're under sovereign rule, just like the rest of us."

Ha Zan grinned and dropped the rag to the desk. "Not anymore." With the snap of his fingers, his guards attacked. Jax pulled a man in front of him to catch the bullets of another's rifle.

Hector caught a sword with his own and pushed back. Another came at him from behind, and though he dodged, a slice across his arm sprayed blood to the floor. He turned and thrust his own sword through the man's stomach. Then he shoved the dying body into another guard, and the man's rifle dropped to the ground. The guard threw up his hands, and Hector held the tip of his sword to his nose. Jax appeared at the guard's side and slugged his temple with the butt of his pistol.

Hector knocked a rifle away from Jax's face, and it went off over his shoulder, making his ears ring. Then Hector punched the shooter in the gut, and Jax shot him through the head.

As Jax continued to fight, Hector spun to the desk and shouted, "Ha Zan! Show your men what kind of king you wish to be. Stand and fight me." The remaining rebels paused, their eyes widening as they snapped back and forth between Hector and their master. "Will you fight your own battles, or send your soldiers to die, as Pollux and Sirena do? Fight me, and if you win, Jax and the others with us will retreat. If I best you, your rebels will back down and let the city elect a new governor, as they have before."

"A governor chosen by the wretched sovereigns," he spat.

"What will it be Ha Zan? Will you keep playing king, hiding in your makeshift castle while those around you do the dirty work, or will you fight for the power you seek to hold?" Hector stepped forward with his sword raised, and the rebel who'd been about to attack him moved out of the way to let him through. Others lowered their weapons to watch. Jax remained on guard, his eyes darting about as he kept track of every person in the room.

Ha Zan tapped his fingers on his blade, considering Hector's proposition. "You seem a worthy warrior, soldier, unlike so many others I have seen wear that uniform. It will be as you say. I will fight you." He stood and rounded the desk with his broadsword. It was wider than Hector's and several inches longer. "I wish to know the name of the soldier I am about to slay, so we may honor your bravery after your death."

"My name is Hector Kayvan, but the funeral taking place today will not be mine." He lunged forward, and their swords clashed. Ha Zan parried and stepped left, but Hector followed with ease. Ha Zan pulled a chair between them, and Hector leapt over it, rushing him and pinning him against the desk. Ha Zan swung with his off-hand, and when Hector ducked, Ha Zan pushed back and escaped. A few more swings had them on the opposite side of the room.

Jax and the rebel soldiers watched, none averting their eyes from the battle.

Ha Zan hopped up on the table and cackled at Hector's surprise. "Shall we make it interesting?"

Hector swung low, and Ha Zan leapt out of the way. Hector used the moment to join him on the table, and the fight continued. They locked blades, and Hector took a fist to the gut. He spun away and blocked a blow from Ha Zan's blade before taking a punch to his face. Spitting blood, he stretched his jaw, massaging it with his free hand. "Are we fighting with swords or fists? Because I'll gladly toss my blade if hand-to-hand is what you prefer."

"All is fair, or so the poets say." Ha Zan rotated and kicked low to trip him, before rising and striking high with his sword.

Hector parried and returned his blow with three quick jabs that had Ha Zan's feet scuffing the edge of the table. "I've never had much time for poetry."

Ha Zan braced himself and pushed back. Their blades connected again and locked hilts. Hector drew his pistol and put a bullet through Ha Zan's chest. The man's eyes widened, his face blanching. "A firearm in a sword-fight? Perhaps you are not as worthy as I first thought, Hector Kayvan."

"All is fair, as you say. It seems your talent to predict the moves of your opponent is as adequate as your ability to hold a commoner's throne." Hector lowered Ha Zan to the table. The rebels in the room stared at him with mouths ajar. "A bargain's a bargain. Flee or be arrested. Fight back and share the fate of your false king."

The rebels exchanged scattered looks before hastening from the room. Hector hopped off the table and wiped bloody hands on his pants as he met his friend's gaze. "Are you going to call me on it?"

Jax shook his head and reloaded his magazine. "I would have started with the pistol and been done with it."

Hector clapped him on the back. "Okay, Blackmoor. Let's go see what kind of trouble Wraith has gotten himself into."

They followed the hall back to the entrance. Jax peeked out first before letting Hector pass by. Dagon and the other Legion soldiers had the rebels on their knees lined up in rows with hands tied behind their backs. No one from the governor's office was there, and Hector assumed they'd escaped through a different route.

When Dagon saw them, he met them halfway across the courtyard. "Is the deed done?"

"It's done. What's going on here?" Hector sheathed his sword and wiped sweat from his face.

"Our insurgents are ready to be transported. Some look strong enough for the farms, but others will be taken to Ashgate, per the King's orders." Dagon cast a glance over his shoulder with a vile grin. "And you know where the women go. The pretty ones, anyway."

Hector looked past him at where a few of the Legion soldiers were already harassing the female rebels. "Let's load them up with those going to the farms instead."

Dagon's brows lifted in surprise, and he tapped his rifle against the palm of his hand. "Those aren't our orders, General."

Hector and Jax shared a look. "Fine. But I don't want any of our men touching them, do you understand? They go straight to the houses, and the brothel madams can handle them from there."

"Understood, sir."

Jax said Hector's name and pointed to the line of prisoners. Hector pushed past Dagon to get a better look. Then he turned back to them. "We aren't taking children, Wraith."

"I was told they go to the madams as well."

Hector shook his head. "No, they don't."

"The fields, then." Dagon glanced between him and Jax, sliding his rifle to rest on his shoulder. "You feeling all right, General? Those kids fought back, same as the others."

"I don't care. We aren't taking them." Hector left them where they stood and began untying the hands of a young girl. She wept in terror. When her hands were free, he ordered her to run, and she did.

Dagon stood with the other soldiers, watching as Hector released four others. "That one was nearly an adult," he complained. "And a fine sight."

Hector's hands shook with rage as he untied another, a young boy of about twelve.

"Shut it, Dagon." Jax holstered his pistol, keen eyes scouring the area for signs of trouble.

Dagon ignored him and approached Hector among the prisoners. "General, our orders were to take them all. The King and Queen will not be pleased."

Hector growled back, "You do what you deem best on your own damn missions, Wraith, but I'm in charge on this one, and I won't be part of this. Let Her Majesty strike me dead if she wishes, but I won't have any more childrens' blood on my hands." Then Hector pushed by him to set the last child free.

Hector stepped into the Hall of Sunsets with Jax and Dagon at his flanks. Pollux and Sirena Aldrich sat on their thrones, elevated atop the golden dais. Commander Rainer was already present, standing before the King and Queen in light discussion. A crimson rug stretched from the door to the thrones, with Watchmen posted on either side every eight feet.

When they reached the dais, Hector nodded to his Commander before bowing to the King and Queen. The sun had begun to set, making it visible in the giant windows behind the thrones and casting a glare off the mosaic tiles of the dais.

"General Kayvan, I hear the takedown at Dysmaa went as planned." King Pollux intertwined his fingers together in front of him. He'd been a military man long ago, though he'd gained some weight since becoming king, making him a little wide around the middle.

"Yes, Your Majesty. Ha Zan is dead, and most of his men were captured, as well as the other insurgents helping them."

Dagon made a noise at his back, and Jax cast him a glare.

Commander Rainer shook Hector's hand. "Making us proud, as always, Hector."

Hector dipped his head. "You honor me with your words, Commander, but I only seek to do what is expected of me."

"I hear he didn't follow his orders to perfection, my King." Queen Sirena crossed one knee over the other. Hector could never help noticing how gorgeous she was—possibly the most attractive woman he'd ever seen—and at times he wondered if it wasn't some kind of spell bewitching him. He didn't know much about the Queen's magic, but he knew she possessed it. Once, he'd considered asking Jax if he felt it, too—that intense desire to stare—but he'd decided against it.

Despite her beauty, she was terrifying. She leveled him with a scowl. "Isn't that right, Hector?"

Hector wiped sweaty palms on his pants as he clasped them behind his back. Swallowing, he latched onto her gaze, forcing his eyes not to fixate on her plunging neckline or hips that filled the throne. "We were to take down the rebel who overthrew the governor and apprehend as many of his soldiers as we could. We have succeeded in this task, Your Majesty."

"But what of the children who fought with them?" She tapped long fingernails on the arms of her throne, her eyes slicing through his chest like invisible blades.

"Minors should not be held accountable for their actions. They know little of the world and only follow the words of those superior to them. They still have a chance at a good life."

"Too true, Hector." Pollux adjusted in his seat and tapped the top of his wife's hand.

Sirena scoffed and yanked her hand from his touch. "I don't see why you favor him, Pollux. This was a direct disobedience."

"Not so, my Queen, but a matter of judgment when in the field, something you know little of."

Her eyes narrowed and looked his way, relieving Hector of her immobilizing stare. "You forget yourself, my love. I know well the field of battle."

Pollux waved her away and returned his attention to the soldiers. Leaning forward, he said, "In light of this successful mission, I believe it's time, Hector."

Sirena choked and grasped the arms of her throne. "Pollux, you can't be serious. We've discussed this."

"Time for what, Your Majesty?" Hector looked back and forth between them, sweat beading on his forehead. His heart hammered in his chest, warming his whole body. He'd tried to please the sovereigns since the day he became a soldier and tried even harder after what happened in Norsukylä. Though he'd known setting the children free might be seen as defiance, he hadn't been able to let it stand. His throat tightened as he waited for his King to respond.

Sirena rose to pace, muttering angrily.

Pollux said, "For you to ascend to the position we've been preparing you for these past years."

Hector's eyes widened, as did the Commander's at his side. Stumbling over his words, he said, "But sire, a new commander isn't usually appointed until the previous has passed or retired."

"He defies you still!" Sirena's voice echoed in the large chamber.

Pollux ignored her and turned his attention to Rainer, who had taken a knee.

"Your Majesty, I have served you well, have I not? I beg you to reconsider. I am still a young man, with plenty of years left in me to perform my duties."

Hector stepped forward. "I agree, my King. I am far younger than Commander Rainer, and far less experienced. While I appreciate your confidence, surely another few years could only help me serve you better as your commander."

Pollux looked between them. After a long moment, his face revealed his decision.

Rainer moved as if to run, and Jax grabbed him, turning him to face the King with his arms behind his back. Hector met his gaze, his eyes alight with panic and regret, and Jax knew immediately he'd made the wrong choice. He should have let Rainer flee.

Pollux looked at Rainer with obvious disappointment. "A soldier should face his death with honor, Commander. You have not lived up to the standards I deem necessary for my Kingdoms. In days of old, a new leader proved his worth by eliminating the previous one. Hector, I leave this to you."

"Sire, I—"

The Queen paused her pacing to shout Hector's name. "You will obey your King, or I will cut your heart out myself. Pollux, already he disobeys you at every turn. How can you seriously believe this is the man to command our Legion? You know the truth of what happened in Norsukylä. You know what a coward he truly is. How can you do this? Why?"

"I see potential where you do not, my Queen."

Sirena stormed toward him, stopping next to his throne and lowering her voice so the others couldn't hear. They conversed in private for a long moment. Hector tried to decipher their words, but they remained just outside his hearing. He thought he might be sweating through his clothing and looked down at his uniform to check. Then he looked at Jax, ignoring Dagon's grin completely.

Pollux cleared his throat and stood. "Now, Hector. Whenever you are ready." Sirena massaged her temples.

Time seemed to stop. Hector's heart throbbed in his ears as he looked from Pollux, to Jax, and finally, to Rainer. As if of its own accord, his hand freed his pistol from the holster on his hip. He swallowed and moved to stand in front of his Commander, who had stopped squirming to face him with a cold glare. Hector heard Sirena say his name again, muffled as if he were underwater. The pistol rose to Rainer's temple. Hector's hand didn't quiver.

"You have earned this, Hector." Pollux stood at his back with a hand on his shoulder. "This is where your path has been leading you. You will be the youngest commander Arkaemor has ever seen, and the greatest. It is written that one soldier will stand above all others. He will do great things for the Kingdoms, like none have done before. I believe you are this man, Hector. They will praise your name for generations to come, but only if you reach out and take what is meant to be yours."

Hector drew in a breath. Then he pulled the trigger. Jax winced and looked away as he held Rainer's body upright. Hector thought it took a long time for the life to fade from Rainer's eyes, but he didn't look away. When his spirit vanished and his eyes closed, Hector told Jax to release him. He wiped blood from his face, smearing it rather than removing it. At the King's pull, he turned. Sirena remained on the dais, a hand on her hip and malicious intent in her eyes. Pollux told him to kneel. Jax and Dagon bowed their heads, squaring their feet with their shoulders.

Placing a sword on Hector's shoulder, then the other, Pollux blessed him. "On this day, the third of Liviana, in the year 4020, I name you Hector Kayvan, the new Commander of the King's Legion."

Orion O'Connell Origins
4013

Orion placed a rock below the hydrangea bushes, brushing its face to remove any lingering dust from the etched words. He snapped the stem of a hydrangea bloom and laid it before the rock, then he stood and wiped his eyes. Looking back at the house, he gleaned every intricacy he could manage, hoping to remember every inch of the building and the grounds. He knew someday he might want those memories, even if he wished to banish them now.

Rather than walking along the road, he cut through a field of corn on his way to the neighbor's stables. His family hadn't been wealthy enough to own a horse, at least not in the past few years, but his neighbors had plenty. Saddling up Molly, an animal who knew him well, he placed a broach of his mother's and the silver spoon his parents had shared at their wedding on the shelf in the stable.

Then he climbed into the saddle and rode southeast. Sylva was only a few hours from the border by horseback, and when he crossed from Reginaterra into Crystavium, he realized immediately that he did not own clothing warm enough to survive the bitter tundra.

Hopping from Molly, he layered up, nearly emptying his pack. He'd taken the rest of his father's whiskey and his favorite flask, and he took a swig from the bottle, hoping the liquor would warm him. Being sixteen, he'd only drunk alcohol once before everything happened. His father had beaten him for it, and he hadn't done it again. Since his father wasn't around now to reprimand him, he'd spent the past few days numbing his pain with the last of his supply. Now he had half a bottle left, not nearly enough to drown the pain for the rest of his life—but a start. He filled the flask and tucked the bottle back into his bag. Then he and Molly continued south.

Crystavium was one of the smaller territories, so it only took a few weeks to cross, but the terrain made it a rough journey. He bought a fur coat and warmer pants along the way, but even with the added layers and Molly at his side, he worried he might fall asleep one night and never wake up. He also purchased another bottle of whiskey from a shady establishment that didn't seem to mind he looked too young to drink it.

When he crossed into Savanni, the instant rise in temperature made him sick. He stopped to rest beneath an acacia tree, shedding his layers and hoping the shade would ease his nausea. After sleeping for a few hours, he and Molly were off again. His coin purse was about depleted, but he'd heard travelers could easily find work on the farms in Savanni, just like in Reginaterra, so he kept his eyes peeled for an opportunity.

After resupplying and selling off his cold-weather clothing in Lupene, he spent three days resting along the banks of Lake Euphony. Or rather, he let Molly rest while he got frightfully drunk and cried his eyes out. On the morning of the fourth day, he saddled up and continued on. They traveled along the Colubrine River until they came across a farm with a sign claiming they were seeking hired help. Though he didn't speak Vetoräti, the language of Savanni, one of the women on staff spoke Arkaen and translated for him. The owner agreed to hire him for a few weeks and told him he could sleep in one of the barns on the property since the houses they kept for workers were full.

The woman's name was Elora. Her skin was as dark as tree bark, like most natives of the savanna, and she was lovely. She walked him around the farm and showed him what he would be doing. She told him he'd been lucky, since the owner of that particular farm was one who didn't take slaves, like so many others did. Everyone who worked for him was treated kindly and paid fairly, but most importantly, they were free.

Orion hadn't known it was customary for farms to keep slaves and wondered if any of the farms in Reginaterra were the same. Elora showed him to the barn she thought he'd like best and left him to rest for the night, promising to return at sunrise to help him get started.

Over the next few weeks, Orion grew stronger. He hadn't realized how weak he'd been until the work began, but already he could feel his days growing easier and his muscles growing hefty. He and Elora spent time together in the evenings, since very few of the others spoke his language. Elora began teaching him Vetoräti, and he was pleased to discover he had an ear for it.

She asked him all kinds of questions about where he came from and where he was going. He kept the details of his past vague and his plans for the future honest—because he truly had no idea what his plans were.

He drank less on the evenings she spent with him, but he found it difficult to sleep sober and usually downed a few swigs as soon as she left. He liked spending time with her, but he couldn't seem to get past thoughts of Lacy Robinson, the girl he'd left behind. He often wondered what she might be up to, or if she still thought of him the way he thought of her. Then he would wash away those thoughts with liquor and flirtations with Elora.

It took him nearly a month to muster the courage to kiss her, and when he had, he'd felt equal parts guilty and awakened. Kissing her made him forget his past almost as efficiently as the whiskey, as did the things that followed—things he'd never had the confidence to do with Lacy.

The bubble of happiness didn't last long. After a few weeks, the excitement of new experiences faded away, and his haunting past returned to the forefront of his thoughts with abandon. He became short with Elora, distant. She clung to him, not understanding his sudden change in attitude. Another three weeks passed before he left in the night and never looked back.

He and Molly continued east, following the river.

Cal'dion was a city unlike any he'd ever seen. The mix of culture and customs had him again feeling that mind-numbing exhilaration. He met many women there, but unlike with Elora and Lacy, he didn't see any of them more than a few times. He'd learned to keep his distance from the start, and that the thrill of someone new was exactly the ticket to stifling his unhappiness. With a new woman each week, and a drink in his hand each night, he hardly felt any unhappiness at all.

That is, until his stifling and drinking turned to fighting. As more space stretched between what he'd been through and where he stood now, guilt and heartbreak transformed into inextinguishable rage.

In a city like Cal'dion, it was easy to find someone looking for a fight. On his sixteenth birthday, he got so drunk he blacked out and woke hours later in an alleyway covered in bruises. After that, it didn't take long for him to move on again.

When he crossed through the barrier into Alunda, the brilliant sun and sandy beaches lifted his spirits. In the port city of Sal, women wore very little clothing and bars stayed open all night long. Still, like every time before, the glitz and glamor of the city only satisfied his fascination for a short time before the restlessness crept back in.

One very late night after too much booze—a new kind of liquor unique to Alunda that was almost clear and tasted like citrus—Orion found himself in another alley fighting three men far more experienced than he was. Hours later, he woke in a haze to the fuzzy sounds of voices.

"This is him, Bells. It's gotta be." A woman's voice, he thought, though he couldn't seem to make his eyelids cooperate.

"You sure? Doesn't look like much to me."

"I'm only following what I'm told, and I'm tellin' ya, he's the one we're here for. Bells, Rosco, pick him up for me, will ya? We should get him to the Peril before he wakes."

Orion shook his head. At least, he thought he did. Then he felt himself lifted into the air, and the black void of sleep overtook him.

Seth and the Niedas
Petal 17, 4023

"Seth! Are you awake up there?"

Footsteps padded the floor above Esther's head until his face appeared at the top of the stairs. He was shirtless and wore only one sock, and his dark hair stood straight up on the left side. "Yes, mama. I'm awake."

"I want you to run out and tend to the chickens. Then I'll make us some eggs for breakfast. What do you think?"

"Okay, I'll be right down." Seth disappeared into his room, and Esther returned to the kitchen to start a fire beneath the stove. Less than a minute later, she heard her son's boots on the stairs. He passed her in the kitchen without a word and hurried out into the rain.

The chicken coop wasn't far, and, living in the Metsa, Seth had grown well accustomed to the near constant precipitation. He liked the sound of the rain pelting the metal roof of the coop, and when it stormed and he knew the chickens might get flustered, he often sat with them to keep them calm.

After feeding the frenzied chickens, he hunted for eggs and found five to bring inside. His mother had already heated the skillet. Dragging a stool up to the stove, Seth cracked them into the pan, giggling at the sizzle as each egg plopped against the cast iron. "Toast, too?" he asked.

"Whatever you want. Why don't you set the table, and I'll get the bread."

Nodding, Seth hopped down from the stool and dragged it in front of the cabinet where they kept the dishes. When he finished setting for two, he sat in his chair and waited for his mother to finish cooking.

"We should go check on Mr. Magpie's flowers today, don't you think?"

"It has been a few days." Seth kicked his legs back and forth beneath the table.

"Knowing him, we may need to water the potted plants in the window sills, too."

Seth chuckled. "Yeah, you're probably right." Esther carried the skillet to the table and scooped eggs onto both plates. Seth scraped butter across his toast, and when Esther sat down, he slid the butter bowl toward her.

Smiling, she thanked him. "When did you get so big, Seth Everett? I thought just yesterday you could hardly walk."

"Mom! I walked fine yesterday. I'm six years old, you know. Of course I can walk!"

Esther rustled his hair. "You're right, you're right. My mistake."

"You're so silly sometimes, mama." Movement outside the window drew his eyes across the room where a blue and gold macaw sat perched in a palm tree. "Are you finished with the parrot painting?"

"Almost." She winked and scooped some egg onto her toast.

Seth liked the idea and did the same with his own. After taking a bite, he spoke with his mouth full. "Who do you think will buy it this time?"

"I'm not sure. I do want to swing by the Myriad Market after we finish up at Mr. Magpie's, since we'll be on the dryside anyway."

His eyes lit with excitement. "Maybe I can get something, too?"

"Only if you do a very good job with the flowers and Mr. Magpie gives you a tip."

"Don't worry. I will!"

C

An hour later, Esther and Seth pushed open the door to the Briar Tavern, triggering the bell as they passed through. Seth carried the basket they used to collect flowers in one hand and a watering can in the other, holding them at his sides as he stomped desert sand from wet shoes.

The owner of the tavern waved as they approached. "Seth, my lad! How are yeh today?"

Seth set his basket and can on the floor and slid up onto the stool at the far side of the bar. Esther stopped next to him. "I'm great! We're here to check your flowers." Though they lived on the Metsa Sateen side of Kesken Ala, Bryä, the language of the Grim Wilds, was Seth's native tongue. His mother began teaching him Arkaen at an early age, and he always switched to the original vernacular of Arkaemor when they visited Mr. Magpie. He'd also learned some Katutaan, the language of the Metsa, though he thought the language of the jungle tricky and tongue-tying, so he didn't use it unless necessary.

"Making a trip into the jungle, eh?" Magpie looked at Esther. "Mighty nice to see you ta-day, Miss Everett."

"Will you ever call me Esther, Mr. Magpie?"

"You call me Mr. Magpie, dearie."

Seth laughed. "That's because no one in town knows your first name. I've asked!"

Magpie chuckled, his hand resting on his plump stomach. "Too true, my friend. Tell ya what? You fill the vases on'a tables and then come back here for lunch, ya hear?"

Nodding, Seth slid from the stool to count how many flowers needed replacing. Esther turned to watch him with her back leaned against the bar.

"You've done a fine job with him, Miss Everett. Don-cha let no'ne tell yeh different."

She smiled at Mr. Magpie over her shoulder. "You know I never listen to the town gossip."

Magpie wrung out a rag and began wiping off the bar. "In a town as small as Kesken Ala, ya can't escape it, now can ya? I just want yeh to know, I'm here fer ya. Fer both a ya, whate'er ya need."

She nodded, her eyes trailing Seth as he scurried from table to table, chatting with the patrons as he went. "I know. He'll likely never know his father, but I'm glad he has you looking out for him. He'll need a man in his life as he grows."

"That he will, ma'am. Yeh ever think of marryin' again?"

"Not in this town. I've met all the men already. Sub-par at best. Except you, of course, but I think Rossnetta might fight me for your hand if it came down to it."

Magpie threw the rag over his shoulder and laughed from his belly. "You watch yer tongue, missy. That's how rumors start!" He continued to laugh, and she joined him.

Seth appeared in front of them. "Three full vases to fill, mama."

Esther bent forward, a twinkle in her eye. "Are you ready to venture into the unknown?"

Seth giggled. "It's not unknown. It's the jungle. We live in the jungle, mama."

"Ah, but there are so many mysteries in the jungle we've yet to discover." She extended a hand, seeking his. "Shall we go on an adventure?"

Seth took her hand and waved farewell to Mr. Magpie, promising to return soon. They followed the main road right down the center of town. Kesken Ala only had one main road. The others were little more than alleys. Passing through the Myriad Market led them straight to the barrier that cut the town in half. One side rested in the desert of the Grim Wilds, and the other in the rainforest of Metsa Sateen.

"Hold your breath," Esther said. Hand in hand, they stepped back through the barrier, feeling it pass over them like a wall of water. Despite standing in the dry desert moments ago, rain now pelted them from above.

Seth shook his hair, already drenched. "It will be better when we're beneath the trees."

They continued on through Kesken Ala until they reached the end of town where the jungle thickened around a single trail. Though tropical flowers bloomed all throughout the Metsa, they knew of a few choice spots to collect a good variety.

Seth led the way, skipping over lifted roots and holding out his hand to smack giant leaves. Esther called for him not to get too far ahead. She always carried a sword on her hip in case they ran into predators, but Seth was too young to be armed with more than a knife to cut stems.

"Hurry mama! We're almost there." Seth turned off the trail and disappeared behind a tree.

Esther rushed to catch up, calling after him. When she reached the clearing, she found him already cutting blooms from a mandevilla. She knelt next to him, and he handed her a flower.

"So pretty, isn't it?"

She accepted the flower and twirled the stem between her fingers before adding it to their basket. "It certainly is."

They spent the next quarter of an hour filling the basket with vibrant blooms. They gathered several varieties of orchids and a few passiflora. The clearing had bromeliads, too, and though Seth always commented on how interesting they looked, he never cut them because his mother had taught him that bromeliads only bloom once. Instead, he enjoyed them during their travels through the jungle and left them be.

As Esther finished clipping a few more orchids, Seth crossed the yard to cut some of the smaller palm branches. Then he heard his mother say his name, and he turned to see her sword drawn and her eyes scouring the trees.

Clutching his knife, he set down the bunch of palms and looked around. "What is it, mama?"

"Seth, I need you to run back to the village. I'll be along right after you."

A chitter at his back had him spinning from her to search the jungle. "Mama, I'm scared." Leaves moved above his head, and he backed away.

"Seth, listen to me. Go, now."

Tears tightened his throat, making him stutter. "No, I won't leave you."

Esther grabbed his hand, and he screamed, just as a monstrous creature dropped in front of them. The ground seemed to shake as it landed on eight spindly legs. Seth stumbled back as his eyes flickered between each one of the beast's own. It had at least a dozen of them scattered throughout its spherical body.

"Seth, run!"

His arm felt ripped from its socket as his mother yanked him away from the monster. Jarred awake, he raced alongside her back the way they'd come. The chittering grew louder as the nieda began its chase. Seth nearly tripped, his eyes blurry with tears, but Esther pulled him on.

A second nieda dropped onto the trail in front of them, and they slammed to stop. Esther pivoted and yanked Seth out of reach as the nieda bit into her arm. She shouted and dropped her sword. Blood poured from the gashes, soaking her clothes. Despite the pain, she swiped the blade from the ground and held it up. "Stay back, beast!"

The first nieda reached them, shoved the second out of the way, and latched on to Esther's opposite arm. Its teeth tore through her flesh, and when it yanked back, her forearm ripped free from the elbow down. She screamed, dropping to her knees as the pain overwhelmed her.

Seth's yell recaptured her focus. She grabbed him, holding him against her side as the niedas backed them into the roots of a giant kapok tree. Esther cut the first nieda longways above its mouth before stabbing it with two quick jabs. It shrieked and backed away, but was deterred for little more than a moment. It charged them.

Esther and Seth dropped to the ground as it slammed into the tree. Sticks and leaves tumbled around them. Esther was losing so much blood, and she could feel her vision blurring as her mind began to fuzz. Getting Seth away became her sole purpose. Her dying wish.

One of the niedas grabbed her leg, its talon-like claws tearing through more skin. Seth hadn't stopped crying. The second nieda grabbed at the first, drawing its attention. The first struck the second, and they began to quarrel.

"Seth, you must run. I will hold them off until you get away. Then I'll follow." She held her severed arm as blood continued to pour. Seth shook his head. "Call for help so we don't have to fight them alone." She squeezed him tight and kissed his cheek. "I love you, Seth." Then she shoved him away. He looked back at her, and she yelled, "I promise I'll be right behind you."

The niedas stopped fighting when they noticed Seth's retreat. Esther stood between them and the village with her sword at the ready. "Don't you worry about him. You keep every one of those disgusting eyes on me."

The first nieda shrieked and charged.

C

Seth was screaming for help before he reached the village. "She needs help! My mother! Someone help her!"

Several young men were gathered outside the butcher shop. One, a man named Daniel, noticed the blood staining Seth's clothes and hurried over to him. "What's wrong, Seth? Calm down, and tell me what happened."

Bryä and Arkaen jumbled together as Seth shouted, "I can't! She needs help. It's a giant spider. Two! Two spiders. Please, help her, Daniel."

The weaponsmith looked at the other men. Some had already darted toward the jungle, needing no further explanation. Others disappeared into nearby homes to grab weapons. Daniel crouched and put a hand on Seth's shoulder. "We'll take care of it. I need you to stay here, okay? Don't run back into the jungle."

Seth shook his head and yanked Daniel's blade free of the sheath on his hip. "I have to help her. I have to save my mom!" He bolted, shoving past Daniel on his way back into the trees.

"Seth, wait!" Daniel rushed after him. Tension built in the village as the commotion drew notice, and several others had hurried off into the jungle to fight. Niedas were not uncommon, and the villagers knew they grew larger in the Metsa than in any other territory. It was imperative to take them out whenever the opportunity arose, especially when the beasts ventured so close to the town.

As he drew closer, Seth heard the horrid shriek of a dying nieda, and his heart fluttered with hope. He sprinted as fast as he could, sure to avoid every stone and lifted root on the trail.

When at last the scene came into view, he watched as the remaining nieda bit into his mother's chest. Her body already hung limp in its arms, saturated in blood and eyes wide open. Gunshots from the attacking villagers echoed in his ears, making him quake. His vision blurred.

Freeing its arms to fight back, the nieda tossed Esther into the closest tree. Her body hit with a crack and tumbled to the ground.

Seth dropped to his knees and wailed. He felt arms around him, dragging him backward, and he screamed to be left alone. "I need to see her. I need to see her. I need to see my mother!"

"I've got you, Seth. You shouldn't see this." Daniel dragged him from the scene.

Seth continued to fight and kick. Then he shrieked, "Mama!" He could no longer see through his own tears. Shoving away from Daniel, he raced back toward the village. People tried to get his attention, but he ignored them. He ran straight down the main street, crossed the barrier into the Grim Wilds, and threw open the door to the Briar Tavern.

Mr. Magpie heard the ruckus and came out of the kitchen to see Seth in a pile of sobs inside the door. He couldn't believe the amount of blood drenching the boy's clothes. Running to him, he dropped to the floor and wrapped him in his arms. "Talk to me, my boy. What happened?"

"They got her. Mr. Magpie. They got her, and I don't think she's coming back." Seth released another wail and pressed his face into Magpie's chest.

The bell above the door chimed, and an older woman burst in. "What's all the—oh, Seth. What on earth?" Rossnetta dropped next to them, her eyes flickering back and forth between him and the tavern owner. "What happened?"

Magpie whispered, "I think it's Esther. Take him, I'll go see what I can find out."

Rossnetta nodded and gently pulled Seth into her arms. Into his ear, she whispered, "You're okay, my child. We've got you. Don't you worry. Whatever has happened, we've got you."

Tunturia Slums
Susi 21, 4018

The house was dark when Raven returned. A fire hadn't been lit in the living room, making the inside nearly as cold as it felt outside. Setting her pouch of tools on the counter, she crept through the shadows searching for her father. When she didn't find him on the couch, she knew he must have gone to bed and made her way back the hall to his room. A familiar metallic smell lingered in the air, making her heart skip a beat.

"Daddy?" she whispered into the darkness. The soft groan of a man rolling over in bed filled her with relief. She backed from the room, but paused at the sound of her name. "I'm here, daddy."

"Did you...?" Raw and rough, his voice came out in a stifled rasp.

"I'll get you more tomorrow. I already talked to Zen. He said Gage has a job for me."

More grunts emerged from the darkness. Raven closed the door and followed the hall to her room. Emptying her purse into the jar she kept beneath her bed, she sighed. Shouts sounded outside the window, then a crash. Raven didn't flinch. She'd grown accustomed to the racket of the slums at an early age.

Tugging off her boots, she slipped into bed fully dressed and pulled the thick covers over her head.

C

The morning sun brought little heat to the tundra. Crystavium was a bitter wasteland. Raven had heard it snowed in Cordillera, too, but that the valley stretching down the middle of the territory remained warm all year round. What she wouldn't give to feel entirely hot from head to toe.

Her father's cough had her pulling off the covers and dragging herself from bed. She already smelled metal in the air. Lighting a fire under the stove, she put on a pot for coffee. Not many in the slums had access to such luxuries, but being a skilled thief had its advantages. She filled a larger pot with water to boil for a bath.

She hadn't bathed her father in over a week, and she didn't think she'd be doing it today, either. It was such a process, and she had somewhere to be. She'd promised to meet Zen before luncheon.

An hour later she stepped out into the snow. Zen only lived a few blocks away. When she knocked on his door, he opened it with a wide smile.

"Rayray, good to see you. I'll be out in one minute." A flame of red hair disappeared behind the door before she could respond. Raven blew breath into her palms, warming her fingers. Zen reemerged in a bundle of leather and pelt. He had no concerns with splurging the little coin they earned. Raven often wondered if he saved a single *aes*, or if it was all squandered on booze and pleasures. At least he seemed smart enough to avoid sil ōnni, unlike her father.

"What's the job?" She fell into step next to him as they started toward the factory district.

"It's big, Ray." Zen lifted his arms into the air. "Huge! Gage told me he needed the best, and I told him I knew just the girl. I'll be expecting my usual cut, of course."

"Despite taking none of the risk and doing none of the work."

"Hey, being a businessman *is* hard work. You have no idea the stresses I'm under."

Raven choked on a laugh. "A businessman? Please. You sweet-talk the hoodrats."

"I make connections! It's called networking. You wouldn't have this job if it wasn't for my smooth-talking. I think I deserve just a little more respect."

"Whatever you say, Zen. You get me the sil?" She lowered her voice as they passed by a shop owner shoveling snow.

Zen sighed and reached into his pocket. "Much as I hate giving this to you, here you go. You can pay me back when the job is done."

"You know I'm good for it. And it's not for me, anyway." She slipped the pouch into her pocket and pulled gloved fingers back to her lips.

"It's not for anyone. It's death to all who touch it. You shouldn't even have it in your hands."

"You just had it in your hands."

He patted his chest with both palms. "But I'm invincible."

Raven shook her head. "You don't have to worry. I have no interest in fading to oblivion. I like my head clear and my senses sharp."

As they reached the street that would lead them to the edge of the slums, Zen stopped and put a hand on her shoulder. "I always worry about you, Ray. Now, keep your mouth shut in there. You're too snarky, and Gage doesn't like anyone with an attitude."

"I've met him before."

"And I guarantee he didn't like you. Just leave the talking to me." He pulled at her sleeve, and they rounded the corner where the road opened up to a frozen field jumbled with warehouses.

The clashes of metal hitting metal reached their ears, drawing their eyes to one of the active buildings. Many had been abandoned over the years, but a few remained functional. Labor pekkōs with chains around their necks worked side by side with the workman, earning nothing for their toil but two meals a day. At least the men came home with a few *aeses*. Maybe a *mett* if they got lucky and the bosses were feeling generous.

On the other side of the warehouse district, the bustling city of Tunteria towered above the river between them. A bridge stretched from one side to the other, guarded with armed soldiers. Very few residents of the slums were granted entry into the city, but Raven had been there several times for various jobs. About a mile up the river from the bridge, a private ferry carried people across for the right price.

Gage had once told Raven that living on the fringes of the ghetto between the poor and the rich was the smartest place to be. Spreading his arms wide, he'd said, *Slummers to my left and aristocrats to my right, and I've got them both in the palm of my hand.*

Two men stood outside the door to Gage's warehouse armed with rifles. Zen put his hands up, and Raven followed his lead. "Gentlemen, I have an appointment."

The bigger man looked back and forth between them. A scar stretched from his left temple to the right side of his jaw. "Who's she?"

Zen said, "She's the one taking the job." The other man chuckled in disbelief, and Raven furrowed her brow. "Trust me, she's tougher than she looks. Now let us through so we won't be late." After a shared glance, the men stepped aside, and Zen dragged Raven through the door.

Streaks of light cut through the boarded windows, creating angular patterns on the floor. Gage sat in a chair at the end of the large room, a caricature of a king on his throne. Raven looked around, scoping for exits, guards, and other threats. So far she counted eight men with guns. Plus Gage, who wore no visible weapon but was scary all the same.

A single pekkō, bigger than the ones she'd seen working outside, stood next to him. It had an iron collar around its thick neck, but no chain tethered it to anything at the moment. She imagined Gage kept it for protection but still wanted the option to restrain it as needed. With a wide, bare chest and long arms hanging past its waist, it almost looked human but for its ashen skin and odd-shaped head. It towered over the guard holding a shotgun to its left.

When they stopped before his makeshift throne, Gage stood and greeted them face to face. He shook Zen's hand before giving his full attention to Raven. "We've met before, haven't we?"

"We have." Raven kept her eyes focused on the center of his forehead.

Leaning closer, he sniffed a lock of her hair. "Was it entertaining?"

"I suppose that depends on your definition of the word."

Zen massaged his temples, shaking his head.

Gage smiled and lifted his chin. "Ah, I do remember you. I thought you were a little young for my taste, but one never knows. You did that Rettko job for me." Raven nodded. Gage looked at Zen and put a hand on his shoulder. "You were right. She's perfect for this."

Zen exhaled, previous energy returning. "I knew you would think so. Just don't forget my cut when it's all said and done."

Gage clapped him on the back and returned to Raven. "You can crack a vault?" She nodded again. "You are to break in unseen and retrieve an envelope from the vault in the master bedroom."

"An envelope?"

Zen opened his mouth to object, but Gage cut him off. "Don't worry, Zen. This isn't a normal job. It's not treasure we're seeking. What I need her to retrieve is important to me personally. Raven, if you're seen, they'll likely kill you, and my chances at retrieving this intel will be gone for good. No mistakes, understood?"

"Understood."

Over the next half an hour, Gage laid out the details of the plan. Raven thought it seemed doable and agreed to strike at nightfall when the master of the house took his mutts for their regular evening stroll.

As Raven and Zen turned to leave, Gage called her name. "Don't disappoint me. I think you know what's at risk if you do."

C

Breaking into the mansion was easier than she'd anticipated. Guards patrolled the front and back of the property, but the side yards were empty and unlit by lanterns. Climbing to the second story window, she wedged a knife inside the crack until it separated and swung free. A single torch lit the room, revealing a lavish bedroom set. Though she often encountered upscale furniture when pulling off a job, this room outdid anything she'd ever seen, and she glanced around to see what else she might pilfer for herself on top of Gage's intel. On the dresser across the room, a hairbrush with a jeweled handle caught her eye.

"Vault first," she said out loud. Gage had told her the vault would be in the floor, hidden beneath the rug at the foot of the bed. Pulling back the rug, she saw a metal square with a standard vault dial, the kind she'd cracked many times before. She got to work, listening for the clicks.

By the time she heard the paws thundering down the hall, the door opened and two dogs rushed in followed by a man in a fur coat. Raven rolled away, hiding on the other side of the bed before sliding beneath it, but the dogs had already noticed her. Their barks and snarls had her covering her ears as a hand grabbed her from behind and yanked her out from under the bed.

The man in the fur coat stood in front of the vault, staring at her. The dogs continued their frantic assault on her ears. "*Tacae.*" The word was sharp like a curse, and the dogs settled in an instant, whimpering briefly as they laid down in a corner of the room.

Raven heard the footsteps of two more men, but they remained behind her and out of sight.

"Catch yourself a stray, Malcolm?" one asked.

Malcolm scratched the scruff of his chin, his eyes shifting between her and the vault. "What do you seek? You are one of Gage's girls?"

Raven glared at him. "I'm no one's girl."

The man clutching her collar shook her. "Respect, you little rat."

Malcolm lifted a hand to settle his guard. "She's fine, Ace. Do you know who I am, girl?" Raven nodded. "Wonderful. Here's the deal. You will tell me the truth, and depending on what that truth is, I will either kill you or set you free. Do you understand?"

Raven threw her head back, cracking Ace in the nose. He released her with a cry, and she scrambled toward the window. The other two men were on her in moments, each holding one hand behind her back. The dogs did little more than lift their heads to watch.

"Feisty, aren't you?" Malcolm said.

"Let me go. I've taken nothing."

He hummed. "Search her, Boris." One of the men took over holding both arms, though he kept his face a fair distance from her head.

Boris stood in front of her, his fingers caressing her sides. His grin made her skin crawl, as did his hands when they lingered over areas no one had ever touched. Sticking two fingers in her pocket, he pulled out the pouch Zen had given her earlier in the day. She'd planned on taking it to her father before darkness fell, but she hadn't been able to make herself return home. "What's this?" Boris held the pouch to his nose and sniffed. "Malcolm, girl's got sil on her."

"Does she now?" The head of the house crossed the room and took the pouch from his hand. "Is this what you were looking for? Funds for your filthy habits?"

"Filthy habits that destroy this city because of rich criminals like you." She spit on the ground, and the men chuckled.

"I see." Malcolm pulled a glass bowl from a drawer by the bed. Yellow film coated the edges, and when she saw it, Raven began to squirm. The grip on her arms tightened.

"Please, don't. It's not for me." Her eyes welled with tears she could do little to stifle.

Malcolm pulled a stick from a jar on the dresser and held it to the torch on the wall. Boris handed over the pouch and stepped out of the way as Malcolm moved to stand in front of her. Holding the stem, he dumped powder into the glass. Then he held the flame to the bottom until it began to smoke.

Raven felt the men's escalating anticipation, their excitement for what followed. She continued to squirm, holding her breath as Malcolm lifted the bowl to her nose. She shook her head, and Malcolm nodded for Boris to hold her still. Giant hands grabbed either side of her face. Malcolm waited patiently for her to run out of breath. When she at last sucked in air, he smiled a fiendish smile.

"There you go. That's a good girl."

Raven's nose filled with metal. She could taste it on her tongue and already felt it infiltrating her senses. She tried to pull away, but Boris and the other guard held her tight. When she began coughing, sending staggering aches into her brain, Malcolm pulled the bowl away.

"Now, the truth, girl. Are you one of Gage's, or do I have to kill you?"

She tried to clear her throat, but it burned, and the acidic taste turned her stomach. "He sent me, yes," she croaked.

"That's what I thought. He wants what I have in that vault. You see, there's nothing valuable in there but the information that holds power over his entire operation. You think Gage rules the slums, but I rule Gage. Now, I'm going to set you free with a message for him. You tell your keeper for me: he's finished. I'm coming for him with everything I've got."

"Why would you warn him?" Raven coughed again, her head swimming.

Malcolm leaned closer and grabbed her chin. "Because I'd like to watch him thrash about like rats in a barrel." Stepping away, he brushed his hands together as if expelling dirt. "Would you like some more of your sil before you go?" Raven tried to shake her head, but Boris held it tight. "You might soon wish you'd given a different answer. Boys, don't have too much fun with her, all right?"

The men chuckled with vile delight as Malcolm left the room, calling for his dogs and closing the door behind them. Boris released her head and moved to stand in front of her again. Ace stood next to him, blood dripping from his nose. Both men looked at the man standing behind her, and Boris nodded.

Suddenly released, Raven stumbled into Ace. He pushed her into Boris, who shoved her to the floor. The men laughed, and Ace kicked her stomach. She rolled from the impact and was met with another boot. She tried to clamber away, but the men were on her, kicking her face, her back, her ribs. Tears spilled down her cheeks. Then Boris was on his knees. He punched her jaw before grabbing her wrists and pinning her to the floor. He said Ace's name, and she felt the transfer of hands. Ace held her wrists so Boris could touch her freely. She tried to kick him, but he straddled her, and when she screamed, he covered her mouth with his hand.

Hours later, Raven heard her name somewhere in the distance. Her head felt foggy. Her legs trembled as she walked, bracing herself against the wall of a building. She didn't know how far she'd traveled, only that she had to keep going; had to get as far away from Malcolm's mansion as she could; had to get somewhere safe.

A hand on her shoulder had her collapsing against the wall. Again she heard her name, and she opened her eyes to see Zen standing over her.

"What the hell happened to you, Ray?" He tried to help her to her feet, but she pushed him away. "Did Malcolm do this? Raven, talk to me."

"Just stay away from me, Zen. Don't—" She coughed and blood sprayed the snow. "Don't touch me."

Zen lifted his hands. "You got it. But talk to me. What happened?"

"I failed. That's what happened. Failed and paid the price." Her body slumped to the cold ground.

"Come on, let me help you. We have to talk to Gage."

Raven shook her head and let it fall against the wall. "I can't. Not like this. Tomorrow. I'll go see him tomorrow."

"No, Ray. He needs to hear about this right now. What if Malcolm strikes back?"

"He plans to. He sent me with a message. Otherwise, I'd be dead."

Zen grabbed her arm and pulled her to her feet. She cringed at his touch but was too weak to pull away. "Come on, I'll help you. I know he has healers on hand. He'll get you stitched up and taken care of."

They arrived at Gage's warehouse within the hour. The guards let them through the front door without a fuss.

Gage sat on his throne, as he had before. He didn't rise to greet them as he took in the scene. "This doesn't look good, Zen." Raven could feel his eyes on her, but she couldn't bring herself to meet them. "What happened?"

She coughed, wishing her ears would stop ringing. "He caught me. Wanted me to tell you he's coming for you."

Standing, he closed the distance between them and examined her wounds, her torn clothing. "He let his boys beat you." Raven nodded, unwilling to share the grotesque details. Briefly she wondered if she'd ever tell anyone, or if shame would take up residence in her heart for the rest of her life.

"You can fix her up, can't you boss?" Zen asked.

"Sure, we can fix her up."

Gage's backhand caught her off guard. The strike tossed her to the floor, and she scuffed her hands on the concrete. A pain in her wrist made her wince, and she thought it might be broken. When she tried to stand, a boot cracked her in the ribs.

Zen's shout preceded the sudden blast of a bullet leaving its chamber.

Raven covered her ears and looked around to find Zen on the ground next to her, eyes wide open and a hole through his forehead. She screamed, and Gage called for his guards to take the body.

Moments later, shouts were heard outside the door. Then three men walked in with weapons raised. "What's going on in here?" one of them shouted. His voice echoed in the large room.

"No business to Legion scum, is it?" Gage called back. The soldiers pressed forward, and as they drew closer, Gage holstered his pistol and lifted his hands. "This is personal business. It's got nothing to do with the King's Legion."

"You handle all of your personal business like this?" One of the soldiers gestured to Raven. She'd given up trying to crawl away and had let her head come to rest on the cool floor.

"As I said, it's no business of yours how I handle my affairs."

Raven felt herself lifted from the ground. Instinct told her to fight back, but she was in too much pain and far too tired to do so. If these soldiers meant to kill her, then so be it. She welcomed the possibility.

"I'll be back for you," the soldier carrying her said.

Gage scoffed. "I'll be waiting, scum."

C

Raven woke sometime later, having no idea how much time had passed or where she'd ended up. She tried to look around, but her eyes were nearly swollen shut. A smell reached her nose, some kind of cooking meat. Her stomach felt instantly ravenous. Then came the excruciating pain covering every inch of her body.

The reminder had memories resurfacing, and her eyes filled with tears.

"You're safe."

The unfamiliar voice shocked her back to awareness, and she searched the room for its owner. When she saw a man in red and gray standing over her, she backed away until she hit the wall. Only then did she realize she lay in a bed. "Where am I? What are you going to do to me?"

"You're in my room at the Caribou Lounge. And as I said, you're safe." He set a steaming mug on a stand to her right. "Try to sit up and sip on this. It's only water, but it's warm."

Raven's eyes darted about, taking in all she could as she began to rise. Everything hurt, but she managed. "Who are you? Why are you helping me?" She looked up at him, squinting in the torchlight. He didn't look like any soldier she'd ever seen, despite his uniform. Hair black as hers was slicked back over the top of his head, and tattoos covered his arms to rolled-up sleeves.

"Name's Jax." He picked up the mug and held it out to her.

She took it, realizing then that he'd wrapped her wrist. Since she could move her fingers, she thought it must not be broken, but it was weak. She pulled the mug closer to let the steam warm her face. "Raven."

"I stitched you where I could see, though I'll be honest, it's not one of my better talents."

"Thanks." She squinted in the dull lantern light, her head still ringing with the aftereffects of sil ōnni. She thought the high had passed, but in her exhaustion, she couldn't be sure.

Jax stood and crossed the room. A few minutes later, he returned with a plate and set it on the bed next to her. "Hungry?"

"Starving." Raven picked at the food while Jax pulled a chair up next to the bed. Sharp eyes followed his every movement. Though she couldn't say why, her gut told her she could trust him. His uniform should have had her cowering in a corner, but the man wearing it had likely saved her life. She'd never seen a Legion soldier save anyone. Certainly not someone as insignificant as her.

"So, do you want to tell me what you were doing at a place like Gage's? You look too young to be pulling jobs for the likes of him."

"I'm seventeen. And who are you to talk, babyface?"

Jax laughed and scuffed his jaw. "That doesn't answer my question."

Head down, she looked up at him through her lashes. "My dad is sick. Mom died awhile ago. I guess things have gotten a little out of hand."

Nodding, he leaned back in his chair and crossed his arms. Her eyes followed the lines of his tattoos. Then he said, "You smell like sil."

Raven sucked in a breath as the memories harassed her again. "Not by choice."

"Gage?"

She shook her head. "Malcolm."

"Damn, girl. You run with a rough crowd, don't you?"

"Said the Legion soldier."

Chuckling, he shrugged. "You should consider joining."

Raven scoffed. "You kidding? Me? In the King's Legion?"

"Why not?"

She looked around the room as if she could see through the walls and all that lay beyond. "You forget where you are, soldier. This is the Tunturia slums. No one crosses that bridge."

"I have a feeling that's not true for you. You're telling me you've never seen the city?"

Her lips curved into a small smile. "Well, maybe not *no one*, I suppose."

He laughed again. "Legion soldiers come from all over Arkaemor. I'm heading back to Inaravale the day after tomorrow. You're welcome to travel with me."

Raven locked eyes with him, feeling the phantom hands of those who'd touched her just hours ago.

Jax seemed to read her fear. "I won't be traveling alone. Two others are coming back with me. One is female. She's nice, for Legion scum." He grinned.

She looked at the food in her lap. "I can't leave my father. Thanks for the offer though."

"I understand." Jax stood and slid the chair back under the table. "I'm going out for a while, but you'll be safe here. Stay as long as you like. Eat, rest." He headed for the door, stopping with his hand on the knob. "Be careful out there."

The moment the door closed behind him, tears consumed her.

C

When she at last ceased sobbing, Raven left the soldier's room and headed out into the street. The first glimmer of daylight had struck the atmosphere, already snuffing out some of the stars. She hobbled up the road, sticking close to the edges in case she lost her balance.

The house was dark when she entered, which came as no surprise. She remembered only when walking through the door that she'd promised to return with sil ōnni for her father. She'd have to find some more when she could move properly. Hopefully his body would survive the withdrawal until then.

Memories of Zen's corpse slumped next to her, eyes dead as a fish, had her grabbing the counter and vomiting on the floor. Then she made her way back the hall and cracked open the door to her father's room. She called out to him with no response. As she crept deeper into the room, she listened for the sound of his breathing. "Daddy? I'm back, but I don't have what I promised. I'll get you more soon, okay? I'm sorry." She stopped by the bed and reached for him. Her fingers landed in something wet. "Daddy?" She felt around for his face, willing her eyes to see in the dull light of the rising sun. Her finger grazed a gash across his throat, and the truth hit her like a brick. She crumpled to the floor beside him and sobbed.

She cried for hours, until the sun was high in the sky. When her tears subsided enough for her to breathe, she covered his face with the blanket and left the room. She packed a bag, stuffing it with everything she could fit. Dumping her jar of coins into one of the outer pouches, she tossed the jar to the bed and shouldered the bag. As she walked the hall to the kitchen, she looked around for anything else she might need.

Then she said farewell to the only place she'd ever called home.

C

Three months later.

"Soldiers! Stand at attention while I take a look at you." A man in royal red walked the line of recruits with his hands clasped behind his back. "My name is Captain Uōtani, but you may refer to me as Captain or sir, and nothing else. You've made it this far, but today is the day we decide if you truly have what it takes to join the King's Legion. I have a few of our elites here to test you. We'll break into squads and let the training begin, but first, introduce yourselves and tell us why you'd like to join the Legion."

He pointed to the person standing at the far side of the line.

Raven's palms sweat like a polar bear in the desert. Not only was she accustomed to the freezing temperatures of Crystavium versus the warmth of Reginaterra, her nerves had her heart pounding so hard she could feel it in her ears. Why *had* she decided to join the King's Legion?

The man to her right spoke, his voice startling her from her thoughts. "Silas Declanaire. I want to join the Legion to honor my father and support my little brother."

"Admirable, Declanaire." Captain Uōtani moved to stand in front of him. "I knew your father. Good man." Silas nodded. Then the Captain was standing in front of Raven. "And what about you? You're a little small to be a soldier, don't you think?"

"Depends on the job, I suppose," Raven said. A quiet gasp sounded around her, but she held the soldier's gaze. "Raven Nightshade. I'm here to right past wrongs and to learn to fight so no one will ever touch me without my permission again."

The Captain grinned and moved on to the next recruit without comment. Raven released a breath.

The man to her right nudged her shoulder, and she looked at him from the corner of her eye. "Hey, I'm Silas."

"I heard," she whispered back.

"Nice to meet you." He smiled, and she furrowed her brow.

"I guess."

"Something you'd like to share with the class, Declanaire?" Uōtani asked.

Silas straightened, squaring his shoulders with his hips. "No, sir."

"If you plan to honor your father, I suggest you keep your eyes forward and stop flirting with beautiful girls."

Chuckling, Silas dipped his chin. "Apologies, sir."

Raven blushed.

"Now, we'll let our experts divide you into teams. This is Faber, O'Connell, and Amar. Faber and Amar are working their way up to the High Legion, and O'Connell is one of our esteemed Reko Raptors."

"Esteemed?" Faber nudged O'Connell.

"Hey, I can't help it if I'm the favorite."

"Skill does not equal favor."

O'Connell shrugged. "Must be my pretty face then."

Raven scoffed and the noise drew everyone's eyes to her. She bit down on her tongue, cursing her idiocy.

"Problem, Nightshade?" O'Connell approached her with crossed arms. His shoulders were wide, intimidating, but Raven straightened her spine.

"I just don't think you're that pretty." She cleared her throat. "Sir."

O'Connell's eyes widened with his smirk. He leaned closer. "You know, Nightshade, raptors eat ravens for breakfast."

"I hear slumrats don't taste very good, but you're welcome to test the theory." Again she bit down on her tongue, holding it there until it bled.

O'Connell looked back at Captain Uōtani with brows raised. The Captain chuckled and shrugged, and O'Connell scratched his chin. "You know what, I like you. I'll take this one." He tossed a thumb at her, and Uōtani nodded. "Name's Orion, but you may continue to call me *sir*." Raven rolled her eyes as he stepped to the side. "I'll take loverboy, too. He's a little scrawny, but I think I can work with that."

The Captain turned to Amar and Faber. "Divide up the rest of them and let's get started. Recruits, camp will be difficult. It will push you to your limits, but if you survive, you'll come out on the other side as a soldier in the King's Legion. Good luck."

To Rebuild the World
Sunset 6, 4027

Asher lit a third lantern, the two already glowing on the table not enough to see the full extent of his research. Maps and parchment covered the surface, and a book lay open before him.

"I found this, sir." The librarian set a manuscript on the table next to him. "*A History of the Ancients*. Perhaps you will find more answers here."

"Thank you, Edmund." Asher opened it to the first page. They'd been at it for hours. The sun had long ago set, but he was determined to stay until he knew with certainty what his next step must be.

Edmund adjusted his robe and clasped his hands together. "May I get you a coffee, sir? The hour is late."

Asher looked up at him. "I'll be out of here soon. I'm sorry to keep you."

"I would never deny a scholar his research. Take all the time you need." The librarian bowed and left Asher to his work.

"The Ancients, huh?" Asher scratched his chin, his other finger sliding down the book's table of contents. He flipped to a chapter on the Deviation and compared it to the writings in *Jumalan Sana*, a book he already had laid open before him. It didn't match up as well as he would've liked, so he set the book aside and thumbed through his journal until he reached the prophecy about the Monastery of the Morrow. *"They rose once before and they'll rise yet again...All lands come together to repair a grand era, each used in the end to unlock the Elvyra..."*

He scribbled ink across a spare bit of parchment and slid his journal aside. Then he picked up a book he had opened to the prophecy about Arella's Comet. *"Nineteen prophesied comets, and the last is just a couple years away."* He tapped a quill against his chin. "Edmund, do you have anything on Arella's Comet?"

"Let me check for you." Edmund circled to the front of his desk and disappeared down an aisle of dusty scrolls.

Asher read over the end of the prophecy. *"Year of dragons, year of tears, brought with them a year of fears. Year of sleep, and one of old, then marks the year all mysteries unfold."* Setting the book down, he leaned back in his chair with a heavy sigh. "The year all mysteries unfold? You know, I could really use Your guidance right now, Elohim." He looked around as if the Creator might answer.

"I found this." Edmund returned with a scroll wrapped in cloth, his fingers fiddling with the clasped. He laid it on the table, unrolling it and holding it open for them both to see.

"The prophecy," Asher said, and Edmund nodded. "Do you think it's related though?"

"Related to the very vague and obscure questions you've asked me to research? I really can't say, sir."

Asher chuckled. "Fair enough. Thank you, Edmund." Again Edmund dipped his chin and returned to his desk. Asher looked over the artistic graph. Though he already had a copy of the words, this scroll was littered with drawings and fancy script. He saw what looked like eggs falling from the sky, a tree with a nest of roots, a dragon in flight, a person standing before another with wings, a building that could be a Monastery, an outline of the Suola Meri, buildings on fire, and a bit of land with rocks standing in a circle.

He rolled up the scroll and set it aside. "Elohim, I feel like You've sent me on this journey with very little to work with." He looked around at the table cluttered with books and scrolls of histories past. "Well, a lot to work with, but not the wisdom to interpret it."

A minute later, with still no reply, Asher sighed again and leaned over the table, his eyes skimming everything laid before him. Then a lantern flickered out, though no wind had slid through the library. He shared a look with Edmund across the room, but the librarian only shrugged and returned to his work. Furrowing his brow, Asher leaned closer to the ousted lantern. In front of it sat his journal opened to a note from an old friend. He read over the note, searching for significance. *"Listen closely to the words and all will be revealed."* He set the journal aside and picked up the prophecy about the Monastery of the Morrow, reading it all the way through for possibly the hundredth time. "What are You trying to get me to see?"

If you read it carefully, you will know what you must do and who you must face in order to do it.

The voice in his ear startled him, but it wasn't the first time he'd heard it. "Responding at last, Elohim? It doesn't seem fair for You to send me on this mission and yet remain so distant."

I am never distant. I gave you everything you would need to complete this task.

"Are you sure?" He continued to scan the ancient words, hunting for secrets woven within them. Then a thought struck him, and his mouth dropped open. "The childson? But...it can't be." When Elohim didn't answer, Asher pressed, "The Prince of Arkaemor must forfeit his crown? *To rebuild the world, it must first be torn down.*" He looked around the room again, wishing he could see the invisible voice, though knowing he never had and likely never would. "You're sure that's the only way, Elohim?"

Another breath of air rustled the parchment on the table. *As the prophets claim, so it shall be.*

Bonus Story: Prince Alexander and His Juliette
Storm 10, 4021

"Your hair looks beautiful today, Nellie. I've never seen you wear it like this." Alexander lifted a coil of dark hair off her cheek, grazing her fair skin with the back of his knuckle. His other hand rested against the wall at her back.

Nellie blushed, her eyes shifting from his to the crimson rug spanning the hall. "Thank you for noticing, Prince Alexander."

"How late are you on duty today?" He grinned, bright eyes dripping with charm.

She drew back, embarrassed, and her words grew quiet as she repeated his name. "I—"

"Alexander."

His father's voice had the Prince turning to face the King of Arkaemor. Nellie hurried off, and Alexander didn't bother to watch her go. "Father, lovely to see you."

"I'm certain I've asked you not to flirt with the castle staff. Though I don't know why I expect you to behave differently after all these years." King Pollux straightened the front of his coat, plucking a piece of lint from his chest. "Where are you off to?"

Alexander clasped his hands together behind his back. "I'm heading into the city to visit a friend."

His father lifted a brow. "A friend, you say? I wasn't aware that the Prince of Arkaemor had any friends. Only consorts."

"Father—"

The King silenced him with a hand in the air. "Have you finished your studies today? Have you done anything at all productive this week?"

"I complemented Nellie's new hair style."

King Pollux snapped his name so sharply, Alexander winced. "That's enough. You know what is expected of you."

"I don't see why I must memorize the laws and regulations. You and Mother will likely live forever, so what's the point? I'll never sit on the Thrones no matter how many hours I spend hunched over a pile of books."

"Perhaps if you knew them more thoroughly, you would break them less."

"Doubtful," Alexander mumbled.

Pollux cleared his throat, an intentional pause to keep his temper. "Your mother and I have been discussing setting you up somewhere else if you can finally prove yourself capable of behaving properly. You could govern a city in Alunda. You love the beach. Or even Cordillera, if Valerian would agree to it. I know he's fond of you. Then your studies would at last be of use."

Alexander's jaw went slack. Then he swallowed. "You would send me away?"

"If it puts you on a better, healthier path and turns you into an adult, then yes, Alexander. I would send you away. You have such potential if you would only allow yourself a modicum of respect or care for your own future. You like Alunda, and the Valentino's have never quarreled with you. You would have control of your own life rather than being trapped behind these walls you loathe so greatly."

"Trapped behind a different set of walls, you mean, and no longer your problem. I'm twenty-two years old, Father. I'm sick of being treated like a child. And I'm sick of being treated like some piece on a chessboard you and mother can move around however suits you best."

Losing his grip, the King shouted, "You are treated like a child because you act like one!" Then he expelled a calming breath and put a hand on his son's shoulder. "Alexander, I only want what's best for you. If you keep this up, the late nights, breaking the rules, a new woman every week, where do you expect your life will end up?"

"I expect it will be *mine*, and mine alone."

"Is that what you want? To be cut off? Separated from your family?"

"We would have to actually *be* a family for that to be possible." He shrugged his father's hand from his shoulder. Then his eyes brightened. "If I'm forced to leave, would you allow Ava to come with me? If I could take her away from here—"

"No. She's too young to be in your charge, and you've proven you can hardly be relied on to take care of yourself, let alone a troubled girl like your sister."

"She's only troubled because every hall of this castle is laced with poison. Imagine what she will be in five years, in ten, if things continue as they are."

Pollux shook his head and exhaled his son's name. "Please return to your room and stay there. Your mother is distraught, and I fear what the next few days will bring. I need you in your room studying so I don't have to worry about where you've run off to."

Alexander scoffed. "Why is she distraught now? Another governor not obeying her supreme will with perfection?"

Pollux met his gaze, his eyes turned down at the corners. "Actually, I haven't had the chance to tell you. I asked the staff to keep it from you until we had more details."

Sensing his father's demeanor shift, he furrowed his brow. "What's going on?"

Pollux took his time answering. "It's Amaryllis, I'm afraid."

Alexander drew in a breath. "What about her? Is she all right?"

A Watchmen entered the hall and bowed as he passed by.

The King waited until the guard turned out of sight before continuing. "She's…well, son, I'm afraid she's taken her own life."

Heart pounding, Alexander took a step back. "What? She can't have."

"She did, my son. Your mother just returned from Ranta. She's gone, and Sawyer has left us. Betrayed us. The Reko Raptors are finished—banished. Your mother is in a fit."

"No, Father, that doesn't make any sense. Amaryllis would never."

"Sirena saw it with her own eyes. I've never witnessed her shed so many tears."

Alexander took another step back, bracing himself with a hand against the wall as his eyes scoured the floor. "What of their daughters?"

"Foxxglove and Iris were not found. I can only imagine Sawyer has taken them with him, wherever he's run off to."

"He was one of your most trusted soldiers. How could this have happened?"

"I can't say, but what I do know is that I need you on your best behavior while we sort it all out. Please, Alexander. Return to your room, and stay there."

Alexander dropped his chin and headed back the hall toward his bedroom. A book lay open on his desk, but he didn't make it past his bed. He sat down on the end with his head in his hands.

Amaryllis had lived with them at Castle Solís when he was a child. She'd been more kind to him than anyone else in his memory, and he remembered her being consistently happy and full of life. "It doesn't make sense," he said to the empty room. "How could she leave her girls behind? How could she be so selfish?"

He fell backwards on the bed and stared up at the ceiling with his arms outstretched. It only took a quarter of an hour in the silence of his room for him to rise again and peek out the door. Two Watchmen moved away from him, their boots scuffing the red carpet, and he watched until they turned into the next hall. Then he snuck out, making his way toward one of the back entrances.

He'd nearly made it out into the gardens when his father's voice had him pressing himself against the wall. Angling his head around the corner, he saw King Pollux talking to his new Commander, Hector Kayvan. They stood face to face speaking in hushed tones, their profiles shining in the torchlight.

Hector's eyes slid down the hall, and Alexander dipped out of sight, hoping the Commander hadn't seen him in the shadows. When he checked again, Hector had a hand on the King's shoulder, guiding him the opposite way down the passage.

C

Half an hour later, Prince Alexander knocked on Juliette's door.

When she opened it, she found him leaning confidently against the jamb. "You're late."

He grinned. "I know. My father tried to confine me to my room. I broke out as soon as I could. Are you ready to go?"

"Where are we going?"

He leaned closer and kissed her cheek. "It's a surprise."

Juliette rolled her eyes and pulled the door closed behind her. "What did you do this time? Hassling the maids?" She lifted a thin brow.

Alexander chuckled and drew his hood back over his head as they started down the street. "That, and, failed to live up to my birthright, made a mockery of my title, and disappointed him in every way possible."

"So, the usual then?"

"Exactly." He led her toward the east gate, chatting with her about anything she might find interesting since they'd last spent time together. When they reached the gate, Alexander's hooded disguise didn't fool the guard, and he slipped the man a *terra* for his discretion. Then they turned north toward the Amber Mountains.

"You think you can get away with pretty much anything, don't you?" Juliette glanced back at the guard examining the *terra* in his hand.

"Absolutely anything, I believe you mean."

Juliette shook her head and followed after him. It wasn't the first time they'd hiked the trails together, and she wondered if he took the other women in his life up into the mountains.

When they reached the trailhead, he pointed at the three options and asked which way she wanted to go.

Juliette studied the sign, though she'd traveled all three trails on multiple occasions and knew where each would lead. Weaving her red waves into a braid, she asked, "Which way do you usually take your other dates?"

He smiled and tugged at a lock of hair she'd missed. "None of the other ladies I spend time with enjoy the great outdoors as much as you."

She thought that wasn't exactly a concrete answer. "To the overlook?"

"Sure." Alexander took the center trail, which began with a sharp climb up a wall of rocks. When he reached the top, he turned back to help her the rest of the way, but Juliette grinned and swatted his hand.

"I can do it." Pulling herself onto the top ledge, she wiped dirt from the front of her tunic.

"I never doubted you for a second." He smiled his charming grin, but rather than kissing her again as she expected him to, he pressed forward.

The trees along the mountain path were still green, though the cold season would be upon them sooner than seemed possible. Alexander thought back over the previous months and wondered about his father's question regarding productivity. Had he accomplished anything? Did he really care either way?

His thoughts turned to Amaryllis, rolling through memories of all the things she'd taught him and all the ways having her in his life had shaped his childhood. He couldn't believe she'd taken her own life. It had been years since he'd seen her, but could things have really changed so drastically? He'd heard she was sick, but if he'd known the depth of it, he would have visited her. He *should* have visited her. His stomach turned as he realized he would never have the chance.

When they'd walked for a while in silence, Juliette asked, "Are you all right? You seem distant today."

He looked back at her and offered another winning smile. "Everything's fine."

She reached for his hand to stop him, and he turned around. "I don't believe you. The light has suddenly gone out in your eyes."

"What?" He leaned closer, intertwining their fingers between them. "That can't be true. My eyes are gorgeous."

Juliette cleared her throat in an attempt not to be wooed. "They are, but today they're distressed." Alexander hummed and moved to turn from her, but she pulled him back. "I know you keep everyone at a distance. I know it's why you won't commit to any of the dozens of women you spend time with. But I'm your friend, Alexander. You can talk to me. You can trust me."

"I know." His eyes slid up the trail as he thought over the conversation with his father. Perhaps he should take his father's offer and move to Alunda or Cordillera. He wondered whether Juliette would prefer the beach or the mountains. Or if she would even be willing to come with him. Or if he even wanted her to.

"So why won't you?"

"I do trust you. I tell you more than anyone else in my life. Save Vali, I suppose. Perhaps even more than him."

"So tell me about this."

Alexander sighed and ran a hand down his face. "You know, this is exactly why I keep everyone at a distance. So I don't have to have these conversations."

She grazed his cheek with the back of her hand and rose up on her toes until their lips touched. "And I've never asked for anything more than you're willing to give me. But I am asking for this. I can tell something is really bothering you. Share it with me, please."

"This is the price of friendship, eh?"

Juliette nodded. "And since I'm your longest and best friend, you have to lean on me. Let me help you, like you've so often helped me."

Sliding a hand around her waist, he pushed her against a wide oak. "Lean on you?" He kissed her, and she wrapped her arms around his neck. "I love leaning on you." Kisses trailed her jaw.

She said his name in scolding. "That's not what I meant."

"But isn't this way more fun?" He nibbled at her ear and chuckled when she sucked in a breath.

Finding her wits, she pushed against his chest. "If you want more, you'll have to be real with me. It's your choice." Slipping beneath his arm, she continued up the trail.

Alexander laughed and jogged after her. "You're so stubborn."

"You're stubborn. I'm delightful."

"That's true." They continued on in silence, but for the birds in the trees and the wind whistling through the leaves as they drew closer to the top of the mountain. After a while, he said, "You know, none of the other dozens of women ever push me to talk about my feelings. They give me whatever I want. I *am* their Prince after all."

She smiled back at him. "None of them love you like I do, Prince Alexander. Perhaps some day you'll realize that."

He chuckled. "I already do. Perhaps someday I'll feel worthy of that love. And not so terrified of it."

"I *am* pretty terrifying," she agreed.

"Delightfully terrifying." He pinched her hip, and she squirmed and rushed ahead.

"Hey, hands to yourself, buddy. You heard my conditions." She winked at him and tossed her braid over her shoulder.

His laugh echoed through the trees. "Fine, fine. I doubt you'll be able to keep your hands off of me eventually. Especially when we get back home."

"Who says I'll let you come into *my* home?"

"You wouldn't really deny me entry."

"If you're going to keep wearing that brooding expression without sharing the details, then I think I will."

Half an hour later, they reached the overlook and stood side by side as they looked out over the valleys between the mountains. The Whispering Moors were too far off to be seen but for a pale fog between the mountain peaks.

Alexander exhaled a steadying breath of crisp air. Then he said, "Amaryllis is dead."

His announcement jarred her from her inspection of the landscape. "Amaryllis? The woman who was always kind to you when you were younger?"

He nodded and crossed his arms. "She killed herself."

Juliette paused to soak that in. She thought he might offer more details, but when he didn't, she asked, "Didn't she have daughters?"

"Two. Foxxglove and Iris. They would be maybe twelve and thirteen now, I think. Maybe twelve and fourteen. I'm really not sure. I've never met them." He wondered if it had truly been that long since he'd seen Amaryllis. She'd visited the Castle a few times, but only once when he'd been home. Even on that occasion he'd been on his way out and had spoken to her but moments.

"Wow. I'm so sorry, Alexander. That's heartbreaking." She reached for his hand, prying it away from where he'd cross them over his chest. "How are you feeling about it?"

He turned to her, his puckish smile returning. "Like I've shared my sadness, and I'd like that kiss now, as promised."

"You're incorrigible." Reaching for his neck, she pulled him down to kiss her. Then she looked up at him, reading the depths of his eyes. The sun was setting beside them, already touching the horizon, and its light accentuated his incredible beauty. "You'd think a Prince would have been taught better manners."

"You know how much I hated my lessons. I rarely paid attention." He kissed her again before turning to face the sunset. They stood there hand in hand, watching until the last of the sun disappeared beneath the horizon. Alexander shared with her glimpses of how he felt about everything he and his father had discussed. She offered wisdom and support, as she always did.

As they headed back down the mountain, she let him hike in silence without bothering him with questions. At the base of the trail, he picked an orange lily and handed it to her.

"Thank you for listening, Juliette."

"Thank you for letting me in." She accepted the flower and smelled it. "You know, if they do send you away, I could come with you." Her eyes remained on the flower, avoiding his.

Alexander grinned. "And be what? My friend? My live-in consort?"

"Your wife?" Her gaze lifted to his.

Pulling her against him, he kissed her cheek. "That was the shoddiest proposal I've ever heard. Sweating and winded from a strenuous hike. Just after hearing my childhood hero took her own life." He smiled, so she knew he was teasing.

"Naturally, since you're the Prince, I'm expecting a very elaborate proposal. This was just my way of planting the idea." She rose up on her toes and kissed both cheeks, then his forehead.

"And you say *I'm* incorrigible."

"I love you with all my heart, Alexander. I'm not trying to pressure you, but I need you to know that you do have a partner in this life, a real partner, if you want it." She nudged him with her hip as she walked by, and he hurried to catch up.

As they walked the eastern wall of Inaravale, he pulled his hood back over his head. Then he took her hand and kissed it. "So, partner, exactly how elaborate are you expecting this proposal to be?"

PART TWO

OF PROPHECY AND SONG

When They Fell

When they fell, it shook the world.
One land divided in two.
A deviation cut a passage through time
woven into the intricacies of what once was
and what would someday be.
He mourned them.
But He had known their futures all along.
Nothing surprised Him. Nothing ever would.
He saw the cords of time and how they twisted and turned.
Like a leaf on the surface of a river.
Like the wind shakes the trees.
He bound them together.
Created a new, so the old could be dealt with.
To guide them. To restrain them.
To break them, if necessary.
A trail forged at the beginning of the ages.
The stepping stones of time forever set in place.
Nothing could alter them.
Nothing could sway the path.
Not even them. Not even the others.
Not even the fated ~Great King of Arkaemor.

~An excerpt from Jumalan Sana.
Found in the book of Jaeho the navi.

Prophecy of the
Monastery of the Morrow

Arkaemor is a world of mystery and wonder,
Seven realms, with each their own treasure to plunder.
One never forgets lavish stories of old,
But can we remember a history untold?

Reginaterra is where the Queen made her home,
A luxurious castle built on flesh and on bone.
Unhappy in life, so the world they remade,
Giving little regard to the price that was paid.

Captured souls in a prison of sinners condemned,
In the depths of the earth vile Strayed apprehend.
Snared in the wasteland of Crystavium,
A Monastery tainted; corrupt and succumbed.

Norsukylä's haven was razed, set ablaze,
In Savanni, where lions and elephants graze.
Chronicles in ashes furnish memoirs rewritten,
Consumed by the wrath of an adversary unbidden.

The sea ebbs and flows with the wind's gentle breeze,
Much like life that transitions between trials and ease.
Alunda's temple was lost, felled deep below waves,
Did the scholars escape? Or sink down to their graves?

Out in the desert where the Wilds are Grim,
Vallemortis redeems when all hope has grown slim.
By an oasis once thriving in the depths of the land,
An old fortress stands lost and covered in sand.

Continuous rain in the Metsa Sateen
Water cleanses, brings life that's luscious and green
At Lacuna Kaput they took shelter at last
When at Imber, the temple was ripped from their grasp.

Oh, great Cordillera! Oh, grand Jericho!
Home of the Monastery of the Morrow!
They rose once before and they'll rise yet again,
The Creator will prove He transcends all men.

All lands come together to repair a grand era,
Each used in the end to unlock the Elvyra.
A childson is needed to do the unbending,
To unwind the history and bring forth all mending.

To shred all to ruins, he'll forfeit his crown,
To rebuild the world, it must first be torn down.
When all is restored, all will bow to one Master,
Living in freedom; peace and joy ever after.

Year of woe, year of weep,

Year of hope, the bad ones reap.

Year of trials, and one of snow,

Year of knowing, then watch it grow.

Year of rest and year of sorrow,

Of victory followed by the morrow.

Then came the lost, then came the found,

And quakes that rocked and shook the ground.

Year of dragons, year of tears,

Brought with them a year of fears.

Year of sleep and one of old,

Then marks the year all mysteries

unfold.

~ Lyrics foretelling Arella's Comet,
Recorded by Kafki the navi

PART THREE

MAPS AND OTHER ODDITIES

The Royal Families of Arkaemor

Reginaterra and Crystavium, and High Rulers of the Five Kingdoms:
 King Pollux and Queen Sirena Aldrich
 Prince Alexander and Princess Avaline Aldrich

Savanni and Alunda:
 Sovrano Dante and Sovrana Serafina Valentino

Metsa Sateen:
 Raja Decha Narong
 Puteri Kirana Narong

Cordillera:
 Konungr Vali and Dröttning Ingrid Kirkavall

The Grim Wilds is *terra nullius*, or unclaimed land, and not ruled by any of the four royal families.

Pronunciations

Locations
Regiaterra	(rah-GEE-nah-TAIR-ah)
Crystavium	(kris-TAH-vee-uhm)
Savanni	(sah-VAH-nee)
Alunda	(ah-LUN-dah)
Grim Wilds	(grim WYE-uldz)
Metsa Sateen	(MET-sah sah-TEEN)
Cordillera	(kor-dil-AIR-ah)
Celestelvyra	(sel-EST-el-VEER-ah)
Arkaemor	(ar-KAY-mohr)

Languages
Arkaen	(ar-KAYN)
Vetoräti	(vet-or-AH-tee)
Bryä	(BREE-yah)
Katutaan	(kah-too-TAHN)

Henki
Orädi	(or-AH-dee)
Driädi	(dree-AH-dee)
Pixū	(pix-OO)
Kukki	(KOO-kee)

Other Creatures
Dimeti	(dye-MEE-tee)
Drakinferno	(drak-en-FUR-noh)
Gnonttū	(NON-too)
Hyvä mon	(HEE-vah mon)
Ignalis	(ig-NAHL-es)
Lepenna	(leh-PEN-ah)
Lunae-lumen	(LOO-nay LOO-men)
Lycanox	(LYE-can-ox)
Nieda	(NEE-dah)
Pekkō	(PEK-oh)
Sandhai	(SAND-hye)
Tinaera	(tin-AIR-ah)
Tryka	(TREE-kah)
Vuokara	(VOO-oh-CAR-ah)

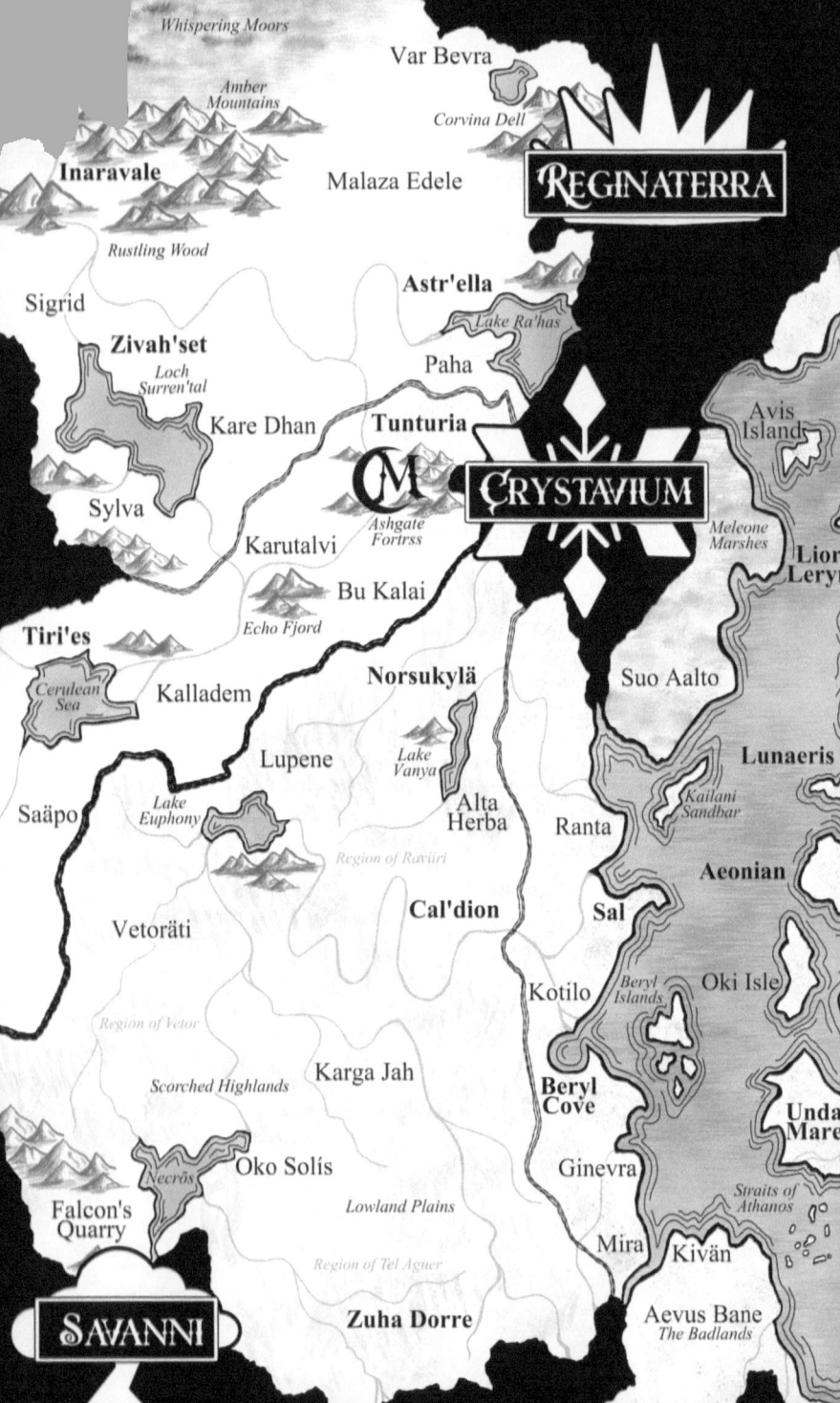

A Year in Moons

Rosh:
is the first month of the year. A time for new beginnings.

Alyin:
means, "halo of the moon."

Sunset:
is the month when you will find the most beautiful sunsets illuminating the desert of the Grim Wilds.

Willow:
is when the willows all over Arkaemor begin to bloom.

Petal:
is the best time to see flowers blooming in the rainforest of Metsa Sateen.

Susi:
is when the arctic wolves are born in the tundra of Crystavium.

London:
honors the first Monastery of the Morrow, which was built in Jericho, Cordillera.

Storm:
is the stormiest month above the Suola Meri in Alunda.

Ammil:
marks the beginning of the cold season in Reginaterra. The leaves change and fall, and it remains cold through Liviana. Then in Rosh, new growth brings green back to the territory.

Reaping:
is the month when the harvest begins.

Navi:
honors the prophecy of the Great King and the Seer, which originated in Savanni.

Liviana:
means, "white moon," and marks the end of the calendar year. The full moon is celebrated in Liviana to honor the Creator.

Nieda

seriously gross

ᐯ

Giant, disgusting spider beast, eight legs, eagle claws,
blue blood, horrific chitter

Poisonous, but curavenum made from their..juices?
Foxx's scar remains dark (2 years)

(3 years)

(5 years...)

segmented
legs

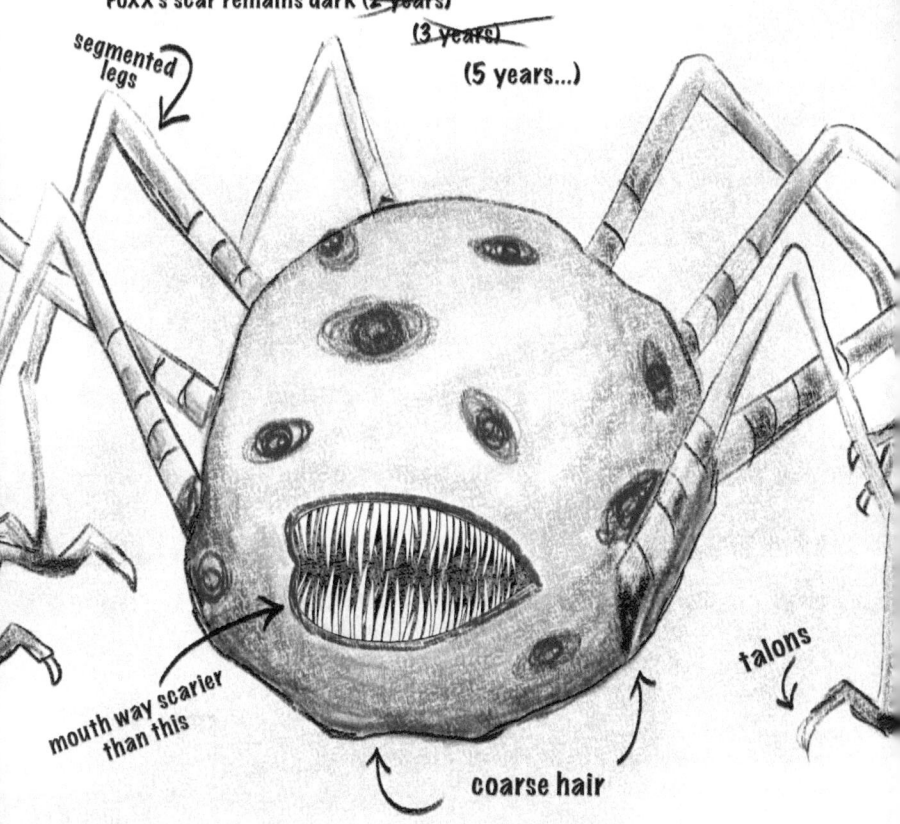

talons

mouth way scarier
than this

coarse hair

Wilds – hair red like clay
burgundy eyes

Metsa Sateen – biggest!!!
teal eyes, light gray hair

Cordillera:
    Cave niedas are afraid of light, are much smaller
than niedas from other territories—though still horrifying—
and have darker hair.

About the Author

Jessica Pietro has been enchanted by fantasy worlds her entire life. Some of her favorite places include: Neverland, Elfhame, Weep, Britannia, Middle-earth, Hogwarts, Narnia, Fiore, Wonderland, and Prythian, to name a few.

Though she's dabbled in writing throughout her life, she never anticipated being a published author. She started her own business in 2019 called Vellichor and More and began selling artwork, unique attire, and home decor. In January 2021, during a horrible season of healing from past traumas, she began writing The Great King and the Seer. Evidence of this is woven throughout the series as her characters learn to love, grow, and heal.

Not only is she passionate about art, writing, reading, and supporting other blossoming creatives, she also enjoys hiking, playing boardgames, studying her bible, watching anime, camping, and spending time with her family.

Jessica resides in Camp Hill, Pennsylvania, with her husband, their son, and their kitties.

Find out more about Jessica by connecting with her on social media. Links to all of her sites can be found here:

https://jessicapietroart.wixsite.com/1234/contact